SPARKS IN THE MOMENT

SEDUCTION IN RED, WHITE & BLUE

JURI HINES

DEDICATION

God, thank you for the gift of expression from my soul to paper.
JaTorri, Alston & Ava, if you want it, go get it. Never let up!
Ma & Dobby, thanks for giving me space to write.
To my family and friends, thank you so much for the genuine support.

SYNOPSIS

Kalyani, a woman scarred by heartbreak, encounters Aeson, a man who embodies her every dream, but carries his own uncertainties. While Aeson is resolute in his life's direction and desires, he must confront his patience in waiting for Kalyani to heal and trust again. As they navigate their kismet connection, will their paths align, or will their individual journeys lead them in different directions? Follow them on a poignant exploration of love, the enduring power to transcend past pain and insecurities, and the courage to seize happiness.

1

KALYANI

"**K**alyani, Mama said get out that bed and gone to the store, nih," my sister-in-law, Eden, yelled through their Face-Time ambush.

"We gotta get the meat cleaned and seasoned, and CP time is not acceptable today. I don't know why you didn't get it yesterday," Daddy yelled in the background. I could hear my mom yelling inaudibly, but I'm sure she was cosigning Daddy. On second thought, she might have been the ringleader.

As they continued to yell all at once, I buried my entire body under my comforter, leaving the phone as an outsider, giving my family ceiling fan views. As a kid, I would always run to my room and hide under the covers whenever I was in trouble. Even when I wasn't the one in trouble, I hid there to make sure I wasn't mistaken for one of the culprits. Some people only required a security blanket; I needed a whole safe haven. I understood the significance of today. The importance of my role in today's festivities. But I truly could not understand why my body would not cooperate. And my parents could not comprehend. Just a month ago, I was happy. Well, maybe not as happy as I wanted to be, but

I was ok. So much had changed from one family function to the next.

Wallowing in my own self-pity seemingly drowned out the noise until I heard a voice, ever so calmly. "Kali, I know it's hard. But Sis…it's for Ma-May."

I simply replied, "Ok," and I got up.

My big brother, Remy, was always my comforter and protector. Being two years older than me, you would think he was the stereotypical bully, but we were polar opposite and best friends. Strangers even thought we were fraternal twins. We were a very tight knit family, and our parents instilled in us to look after one another because we were all we got, and we had held on to that philosophy with all our hearts. Our parents, Amarie and Jamison, worked very hard to provide for us, and unfortunately, like in many black families, working hard required long work hours. As a result, we spent a lot of time with our maternal grandmother, MaryAnn, or Ma-May as we called her. Our grandfather, Mason, had passed away when my mom was in high school, so I never had a chance to meet him. Daddy's parents, Grandma Dot and Grandpa Paul, lived in Virginia, so we only saw them a few times a year. As the baby and only girl, I craved my parents' attention, but Ma-May and Remy filled those voids as best as they could. Being in a large family, I had plenty of cousins, and we always linked up at our grandmother's house for sleepovers, game nights, birthday parties, or even just to sit on the porch. You know that house where all the kids in the neighborhood would hang out? That was my grandmother's house. There was truly no safer place to be and never a dull moment at Ma-May's.

And speaking of, I was definitely running late getting over there. Today was Ma-May's 75th birthday and the family was throwing her a huge birthday cookout. Mama always said that there was no better day for MaryAnn Boyce to be born than on the 4th of July because she was an absolute firecracker. We called our grandmother Ma-May because she refused to be called "Grandma." Homegirl said though she was grand, she was too young to be considered that old. And at 75, she was still in great health and as spunky as she wanted to be. She wouldn't even let us surprise her with a party, because she pretty much had the plans laid out. During our Christmas dinner last year, she presented everyone with her party ideas and told us not to mess it up. And the day finally arrived. There couldn't have been a better reason for me to snap out of my funk and enjoy the day.

I ran to my bathroom and brushed my teeth and cleansed, toned, and moisturized my face. Thankfully, I took a shower after my morning run. I threw on a pink Nike sports bra with matching black leggings and paired them with my black and pink Nike gym shoes. Once I threw my locs into a high bun, I ran out the door and headed to Publix before anybody could call me back and fuss.

Layton traffic wasn't too bad to say it was a holiday, so I hoped the grocery store wasn't too packed either. It was only a fifteen-minute drive from my townhouse to the grocery store and about another seven minutes to Ma-May's house from there. So, I proceeded to my destination while Shae' Universe belted "What's Luv" in my ear. This song had been on repeat for the past few weeks as I struggled to get through this breakup. As affirming as the song was, tears still began falling for the 100th time as she sang, *What's love if you ain't speaking from the heart/Empty promises you should've never started/Now I'm gonna have to love you from afar.* Truly a breakup song. I should have just played, "I'm Going Down" by Mary J. It would have had the same effect. My mind was in the same place that it had been for the last month, leaving me in shambles or on autopilot. In this moment, I was surely the latter, because I was so consumed that I didn't even remember the ride to the store or walking inside. Hence, how I ended up without a grocery basket or cart. As mentally and physically exhausted as I was, I didn't even feel like walking back to the front of the store to get it. I figured it would be ok, since I was only grabbing a few packs of meat, per my daddy's earlier text.

Yet, in true Gibson fashion, my daddy texted me again.

> Dad: KaliBoo, how about grab some seasonings and BBQ sauce while you out.

> Dad: I know you ain't got the meat yet so don't even try to say you already left.

> Dad: If you left, go back.

I rolled my eyes as I looked at the texts, because why does he have to send three texts back to back? He probably used talk to text. And secondly, Ma-May had six children, who all had at least one child. Uncle Gary had five. Why was *I* the one stuck grabbing all the stuff?!

I dialed my dad's number to protest and get somebody else to do it. My mom answered, which was the norm. Daddy would leave his phone anywhere and not have a care in the world.

"Hey, Kali!"

"Hey, Mama. Where's your husband?"

"Outside arguing with your Uncle Aaron about whose barbecue sauce tastes better. The usual." I could hear her deep sigh and felt her eye roll through the phone. Uncle Aaron was one of my mom's older brothers. He and Daddy were best friends since they were kids, so they were more like brothers than in-laws. They bickered like kids about everything from who was the better cook to who had the lowest cholesterol.

"Well, I guess that answers my question about his add-ons to the list. But why do I have to get it?" I whined.

"Kali, you're in the store! Just get the stuff and come on! Had you handled your business earlier, you would have been free from store duty. So don't blame anybody but yourself. Come on, nih. We're all just waiting on you and time is ticking." And with that, she hung up. A few seconds later, my Cashapp went off. Mama sent me $250 with a subject of, "For your troubles," with the winking and kissing emoji.

My mom was truly a hard ass, but she knew how to soften the blow. She was right, as usual. I could have and should have gotten everything I needed the day before, as I intended, but I fell in my funk and couldn't muster the energy to do it. Using Instacart crossed my mind, but I preferred to pick my own meat and produce. One thing about depression, that bastard didn't care what was on the schedule.

I continued to play my music in my air pods as I proceeded down the aisle to get the seasonings and sauce. I figured I could pile everything strategically in my arms because I really didn't want to walk back to the front of the store. I was hoping to find an abandoned cart nearby, but of course, these things never happened when you needed them.

2

AESON

My first Fourth of July in a new city, without my family…
and groceries. I mean, I had the basics: cereal, noodles,
ice cream, fruit for my protein shakes, and my favorite salt and
pepper chips. I even had a few Zatarains alfredo bowls in the
freezer. But who wants that on The Fourth? My palette was
craving grilled food. More specifically, a burnt hot dog. And I
didn't even own a grill. Guess it was time to go get one.

Two months ago, I relocated to Bay Springs for a great job
opportunity with a software development company. In my
attempt to get situated I hadn't really had an opportunity to meet
many people other than coworkers. The few I'd met have been
pretty cool so far. They even took me out for drinks to welcome
me to the team. I instantly clicked with one of the engineers,
Remy. I was a couple years older than him, but we shared a lot of
similar interests. He graciously offered to show me around the
area and even connect me with a potential barber. Although I had
been growing my locs for the past six years, I cut them off and
went back to the low Caesar as part of a new beginning, so I had
to keep the waves fresh. There were a couple braiders and locti-

cians in the shop so if I ever decided to grow my hair back out, I'd have someone nearby to reattach them. Until then, the locs would stay in the bag in my closet.

Bay Springs was a small town, but I still had to use my GPS most of time. If it wasn't within the pathway of home to work, I probably would get lost. Though the town gave southern home vibes with the brick homes lined with trees, it was developing into a flourishing enclave. And anything that couldn't be found in Bay Springs could be found minutes away in Layton.

"Siri, give me directions to Home Depot."

"Getting directions to Home Depot," she replied. And we were on our way.

Twelve minutes later, I arrived at my destination. I felt like I hit the lottery once I saw Publix in the vicinity. That meant less driving for me. Since it was the Fourth of July, Home Depot had a nice sale going. I purchased my heavy-duty stainless steel charcoal grill, an extra large bag of charcoal, and headed back to my truck to load the grill before going inside Publix. Considering it was just me, I didn't need much, but whatever I cooked would have to last a couple days. I placed some fresh asparagus and corn on the cob into my shopping cart and headed towards the meat section. There wasn't a huge selection to choose from considering it was the holiday. Most people prepared ahead of time, leaving us stragglers to pick over what was left. I managed to grab a tray of pork chops, wings, sausage, and hot dogs, which would be more than enough for me.

I headed to the register, but doubled back once it hit me that I was out of my Slap Ya' Mama seasoning. I would've been highly upset if I made it all the way home without it and had to come back out. As I made my way down the aisle, I noticed a beautiful woman with no buggy, but an arm full of groceries, still reaching for more. I didn't understand why women think they could carry everything. Or even should have to do so. As she attempted to reach for some barbeque sauce, her items started to fall out of her arms. I ran over to her to catch what I could before they hit the floor.

"Hey, looks like you could use a little help. You good? Do you need me to get you a buggy?"

"No, I'm fine. This was the last thing I needed. Thank you though," she stated, but her eyes said something different. As we stood there silently, for what seemed like forever, I noticed just how beautiful she was. She stood shorter than my 6'2" frame, at about 5'5" if I had to take a guess. Her skin was a caramel brown complexion with soft freckles across her nose, and her full lips were pink and glistening from her lip gloss. In all her natural beauty, her almond eyes were glossy with a glimpse of sadness lying underneath. Her locs were in a high bun with a couple of them adorning the sides of her face. I noticed many piercings embellishing her ears, from the big gold hoops to the studs and a nose ring. As I gave her body a full overview, I noticed her fit physique in her yoga outfit. Her body was giving all-natural, giving Megan the Stallion vibes.

I had to break myself out of the trance and suggested to her, "Ok, well since we're both done, let me at least give your groceries a ride to the register. You look like you're carrying the weight of the world in your arms instead of on your shoulders."

She tilted her head slightly to the left and squinted her eyes as if trying to read into my motives or even my soul, contemplating if my intentions were pure or if I was running game. As beautiful as she was, the sadness in her eyes was my red flag. She had her own shit to work out, and honestly, I wasn't the type for drama. Before she could object, I began grabbing the meat, seasonings, and sauces out of her arms, placed them in the buggy, and headed towards checkout.

As the young cashier checked us out, I stated, "Ring them up together, but bag these separate from those," pointing at the items on the conveyor, indicating which was which.

"No!" she nearly yelled. "I couldn't ask you to do that. I can cover it." And she attempted to pull out her debit card.

"Good thing you didn't ask. And neither am I. It's cool," I said with a smirk. She relented, but I could see the stress lines forming across her forehead. The cashier's eyes shifted back and forth watching the exchange as though it was a tennis match. After paying for the items, I returned the cart and proceeded to carry them all out of the store.

"Would you like for me to take them to your car?"

"No, you've done quite enough. Thank you so much. Again, you really didn't have to do this."

"Again, it's cool. Besides, you seem like you needed a win today." I stated with a smile, as I handed her the three bags with her items.

"Oh wow. I didn't realize it was that obvious," she stated, looking towards the ground. "Well, thank you again."

"You're welcome, Beautiful. Enjoy your holiday."

"You, too."

I wanted to watch her to ensure she made it to her vehicle safely, but I didn't want to give off stalker vibes, like a predator, so I headed back to my truck. I was far from that. My mama just raised me right. She taught me to look after every woman, especially our black women, as though they were my responsibility. Because they were. If not for her sad aura, I would've shot my shot, but every opportunity was not always the best opportunity. Plus, Cutie clearly needed to work out some unresolved issues. As I cranked up my truck and headed back home, "Can We Talk" by Tevin Campbell belted through the speakers. Then it hit me. Damn, I could've at least asked her name.

3

KALYANI

W hat in the hell just happened? That fine ass man left me stuck and confused. Ten minutes later, I was still sitting in Publix parking lot, trying to get my bearings. I was not expecting to run into a man like that when I left home. I only expected to grab what I needed and be on my way, not to be smitten over a man who was simply helping me with my groceries. And a fine man at that. Scratch that, that man was beautiful. At first glance, I could've sworn I saw a golden light shining around him like Patrick Swayze in *Ghost*. His tall, medium built stature towered over me at about 6'2". His teeth were extremely white against his deep chocolate skin. It was more like Sepia and bronzed. And his smile…those dimples…my heart bounced on the pit of my stomach like a trampoline.

During this brief interaction, I forgot all about the depression I felt all morning and the frustration from running this errand. Feeling his genuineness brought a sense of peace over me. I felt like I could breathe, but at the same time, I was holding my breath anticipating his next word. As he handed me my bags and I walked to my car, I finally exhaled. I threw my bags in the backseat of my Chevy Blazer, and I sat in my driver's seat and proceeded to press the start button when a thought hit me. He was the true definition of a gentleman. He wanted nothing from me but to help me. Even after paying for my items, he didn't make any snide remarks, didn't look at me perversely, or make any sexual innuendo. And with that thought, I immediately burst into tears. Not because he didn't ask me for my number, but because someone just wanted to *be there* for me. He noticed that I needed a win, and he gave me that so selflessly. He didn't criticize me or make me feel stupid for not grabbing a shopping cart. He didn't let me struggle or wait for me and my items to hit the floor. And that melted my heart. And for *that,* I cried. Because someone gave me the basic treatment that any person should receive without me owing them something in return. And that was so abnormal for me that I became amazed. I was so accustomed to Lucas's ridicule that this strange man amazed me at Publix. How sad was I? Oh, God! Did he help me out of kindness, or was it an act of pity? Now I cried because I was truly pitiful. Mr. Sepia saw my pitiful ass struggling and felt sorry for me. He didn't even bother to ask for my name or give me his. How embarrassing! I cried even harder for the next ten minutes.

Finally composing myself enough I headed to Ma-May's house in Bay Springs. It was a surprise no one called looking for me. It was just a short drive from Layton, but I drove rather slowly, taking in the scenery. I loved everything about the little suburbia of Bay Springs. There were a few stores and restaurants, but the neighborhood stole the show. Ma-May's neighborhood was one of nostalgia. There were tall, full trees aligning the sidewalks with huge lots encompassing massive homes. The area was rather mixed-raced and either elderly or family-oriented. Seeing the children playing basketball, kickball, and hopscotch reminded me of my younger days, and I often found myself reminiscing on all the times spent outside with my cousins and Remy. Although I bought my townhouse in Layton, that was more so because it was an offer I would have been crazy to refuse. My forever home would have to be in Bay Springs.

After parking alongside the sidewalk, I checked the time to see that it was only a little after eleven o'clock. The party wasn't set to start until four o'clock, so I was good. I put a couple of Clear Eyes drops in each eye and used my concealer and setting powder to hide the evidence from my mini breakdown. Walking up the long driveway, I noticed quite a few family members and neighbors had already arrived. My grandparents were one of the first families to move into the neighborhood when it was just a few small houses lining the streets. As the family grew and income increased, my grandfather renovated and added onto the property to accommodate our growing family. Eventually, they purchased the adjoining lot to build a recreational area for family events that we called the "rec room" for short. As well known and loved as my grandmother was, I wouldn't be surprised if this turned into a whole block party. We surely had enough space and food to accommodate everyone. Daddy and Uncle Aaron were still by the grills with a few others, while my other uncles and cousins were setting up tents, tables, and chairs. Kids were running around everywhere.

"Scoot, Manny!" I yelled to my teenage cousins. "Can you guys grab those bags out the backseat and take them in the kitchen?"

"You gonna pay me?" Manny asked.

"Yep, pay your ass no attention! Don't forget I know where you *really* were last month. I'm sure your mom would be interested as well."

Scoot stepped in front of Manny with his arms up in surrender. "Auntie Kali, don't listen to Manny. You know we got you. Ain't nobody gotta know what we know, ya feel me? No need in ruining this beautiful day."

"Yeah, that's what I thought," I replied, laughing as I walked towards my daddy and Remy, speaking to several people on the way.

"Hey, everybody! Hey, Rem," I spoke, as I hugged my brother, and he kissed my cheek. "Where's Eden?"

"Taking a nap. She'll be here a little later." Eden was five months pregnant with my first niece, so I understood.

"Hey, Daddy! The boys are taking the groceries in the house now," I spoke as I kissed him on the cheek.

"Thank you, baby. Let me go inside and mix up my specialty. Don't y'all niggas follow me either. Especially you, Aaron."

All the men were laughing as Uncle Aaron yelled, "Man, kiss my ass, Jamison!"

"Don't be mad. You know I whip up the sauciest concoctions this side of the Mason-Dixon Line!"

They all burst into laughter as I walked inside the house. To say Daddy was supposed to be following me, he was still outside running his mouth.

I stepped inside the huge kitchen to see all the ladies working hard preparing sides and desserts. I greeted everyone with kisses and hugs as I headed in my mom's direction. Kissing her cheek, she cut her eyes at me and commented, "It's about time you got here."

"Hey, Mama. Where's Ma-May?" I greeted, ignoring her slick remark.

"She's still out with Ms. Betty getting their spa treatments. They should be back in a couple hours. Wash your hands and help Zena with that pasta salad that she's been working on for the longest."

"Auntie, why you gotta play me like that?! I'm doing what y'all said, but this is a lot! Y'all must be feeding the whole city with all this food," Zena yelled.

"I don't care how much it is. That ain't got nothing to do with the price of tea in China. Hell, you would think you'd move a little faster since it's so much. You won't stop running your mouth, and you have the attention span of a rock! Ain't it, Jackie?"

"Chile, I deal with it every damn day. I'm off on holidays, so she's y'all problem today," Aunt Jackie cackled while she stirred whatever that was in the tall pot on the stove.

I hugged Zena and defended her by saying, "Cuzzy, don't mind her. I got your back." Zena and I were four months apart, so we grew up very close. Aside from Remy, she was my best friend. Obviously, with her being my age and a girl, our bond was a little different than my relationship with Remy. While he was my protector, she was my instigator. She was the Ethel to my Lucy, the Pam to my Gina.

She whispered to me, "I can't stand your bald head mama sometimes." And we burst into laughter. My mother had been rocking her low cut fade for years, and Zena never failed to call her *bald headed* whenever she got on her nerves.

As we proceeded to cut up the meats and veggies for the multiple pans of pasta salad, Zena asked, "So what's up with you this morning? Eden said you were having a rough time. I was gonna call, but she said Uncle Jay and Aunt Scoop Bald were on your case. I figured you'd call me if you really needed me or otherwise, we'd have a session here at the house."

"This morning was rough, Z. I don't get it. I was doing so good all week. Yesterday was great. The morning started okay enough for me to take a run, but once I got home and actually sat down, all I could think about was how Lucas was with me at the last family gathering on Memorial Day. Now today, I have to go around the same people and save face while they ask me where's Lucas, and still muster a smile while they give me the sympathy head tilt and ask if I'm okay. And just that quick, I was back in bed." I replied while fighting the tears on the verge of falling.

"Girl, Eff them people!" Zena yelled while looking around to make sure none of the aunties heard her almost curse. "You don't have to explain anything to anybody. When they ask where that trifling nigga at, tell them he's with one of the raunchy hoes he cheated on you with, sleeping on their air mattress, and eating their kids' fruit snacks and throwing back Kool-Aid Jammers. Hell, tag me in. I'll tell them for you!"

By now, the tears had no choice but to burst through, but only because I couldn't control my laughter. Zena was effortlessly hilarious, and rarely did she ever bite her tongue.

"Girl, you are a fool!" I exclaimed.

"Got you out your funk, ain't it?" She smirked.

"Yeah, but you're not the only one to better my mood." Now it was my turn to smirk.

"Biiiiiihhhhhh, don't tell me you got some meat before you picked up the meat!" she screamed.

"No girl!" I replied, pushing her shoulder.

"AFTER?! Where? With who? That was quick, ain't it?" She thew the knife and the ham down on the table and fell back in her chair, being her dramatic self.

"Zena, if you don't cut it out and cut up this meat before the kitchen supervisors come in here! If you be quiet, I can tell you what happened. Damn!"

She childishly cinched her lips closed with a zipper-like gesture over her mouth.

"Now, for your information, I did not in any way, shape, or form screw anyone neither before nor after my trip to Publix. The only meat I got was chicken and ribs. I did kinda meet this fine ass chocolatey, loc'd savior while getting barbecue sauce."

Zena gestured over her mouth once again, but this time to unzip. "BARBECUE SAUCE?! The hell?"

I laughed and began recounting today's events while we finished the pans of pasta salad.

4

AESON

I took the grill off the back of the truck and set it up in my driveway as soon as I got back home. I was already vibing to a 90's-2000's hip-hop playlist in the truck so I let it keep playing throughout the house. While preparing my food, I couldn't help but miss my family, especially my parents. My older brother, Reece, moved to California over ten years ago, so I was used to not seeing him. We texted at least once a week to check in, and FaceTimed maybe once a month or so, but I hadn't physically seen him in person since the first anniversary of Mom's passing last year. Pops passed away almost six years ago from a car accident. Early one morning, on his way to work, he was hit head on and died instantly. Unfortunately, the driver fell asleep behind the wheel after working a 12-hour shift. Though he survived and my pops didn't, he suffered some severe injuries that left him paralyzed. My mom never recovered from the heartbreak of losing her husband. My parents had been together since they were fifteen years old, and I admired how they managed to keep their spark alive throughout the decades. They did so much together and made beautiful memories, from attending sporting events to gardening to even taking cooking classes together. As a child, I would watch them both get ready for their weekly dates like they were still teens headed to prom, and we always took their picture before they left. There were so many pictures. Pop's passing was ultimately the blow that extinguished the spark in my mom. Her health began to decline rather quickly. She fell into a deep depression despite all our attempts to keep her busy and vibrant. I even tried taking her out on weekly dates, but after a few months, she said it didn't feel right without her Cannon. Almost two years ago, I went to my mom's house early one morning to cook her breakfast only to find her lifeless in Pop's recliner, holding a photograph of the two of them. An autopsy revealed that Mom passed from a massive heart attack, but in all actuality, her heart had been broken for years. And she was tired of trying to mend it. I recalled a conversation she and I had over breakfast.

"Ma, do you think I'll ever have what you and Pop had? I'm already over thirty. Do you think it's too late?"

She set her fork down, grabbed my hand, and looked into my eyes. "Baby, it's not too late. You're gonna find your one, and she's going to change your world. You're too loving of a man to be alone. Thank God that you didn't find your love at such an early age. Maybe it won't hurt as much when one of you leaves. Your daddy was all I knew."

In an effort to lighten the mood and make her laugh, I said, "I don't know, Mama. If she don't make my egg sandwich right, she gon' have to go. And I'm gonna end up right back here eating with you."

With her eyes glossed over, she gave me a half smile and spoke through trembling lips, "Well, you'll have to communicate. Teach her. Because I don't know, baby. Some wounds are too deep to heal."

With that being said, we continued to eat our breakfast in silence. One week later, she was gone.

I caught myself wiping away a stray tear with my arm and took my chicken, ribs, hot dogs, sausage, and corn to the grill. I had a small pan of baked beans mixed with ground turkey cooking on the stove. It sounded like a lot of food, but I'd have all of this gone in the next two days. As I tended to my grill, I noticed cars piling in at the house across the street. Neighbors were also walking in the same direction, some carrying dishes with them. I hadn't really had the opportunity to meet many people in the neighborhood other than my next-door neighbors, Mr. and Mrs. Taylor, who were walking out of their house carrying two long pans and a big gift bag.

"Hey there, Aeson!" Mr. Taylor spoke as they walked towards the road. I strolled towards the end of my driveway to greet them.

"Hey. Happy Fourth to you both," I kissed Mrs. Taylor's cheek and shook Mr. Taylor's hand. They were an older couple in their 60's who bought their home over 40 years ago. "Y'all headed across the street too, huh?"

"Oh yeah," he stated excitedly. "It's not really for the holiday though. It's MaryAnn's birthday, so it's about to be a time."

"Yes, it is. Aeson, you should come. I know she wouldn't mind. She's got some pretty grandgirls, too." Mrs. Taylor suggested, giving me a sly grin. I believe once she found out I was single, she decided to make it her mission to help me find a wife.

"No, I don't want to intrude, especially without meeting her beforehand and no gift. I'll make sure to make her acquaintance soon though, so I won't miss any future engagements."

"Ok, suit yourself. I'll bring you a plate back," she told me, kissing my cheek.

"Thank you. See y'all later, and don't cut up too bad, Mr. Taylor!"

"Ohhhh, Buddy! I gotta show them kids I still got it. I've been practicing on the tickity toks!"

"I hear you, Mr. Taylor," I chuckled as I walked back up my

driveway to check on my food, still watching all the people file into the party.

I decided to shoot my brother a text.

Hey bro. Happy 4th. Hope all is well. Love ya.

I missed my family.

5

KALYANI

Ma-May's yard looked like a Walmart parking lot. Cars were everywhere. I don't know whose idea it was to hire parking attendants, but it was a brilliant idea. They had the cars parked so nice and neat in the front yard. Cars also alined the street, and that didn't include the guests who walked. Ma-May made it back from the spa and was now in the staging area with her stylist, makeup artist, and hair stylist, also known as her bedroom. And none of us could come in until she was ready. She was so dramatic. That was no problem considering we all worked diligently to perfect the honoree's entrance, the DJ kept the vibes going, playing a wide range from "Midnight Train to Georgia" to "Cuff it." I even heard "Bump and Grind" play earlier.

My aunts, Chanie and Chance, had a very lucrative event planning business in Atlanta, so they pulled out all the stops, decorating the the inside of the rec room, as well as outside. There were flowers and lights everywhere with red, white, blue, and gold balloons and décor. The tables were adorned with different types of centerpieces, encasing framed photos of Ma-May from her birthday photo shoot. There were balloon arches, multiple photo backdrops, photo booths, a bar, and so much food on the buffet line.

"Love Come Down" by Evelyn Champagne King began playing and the DJ called for everyone's attention. "Yoooooooo, it's time to recognize the woman of the hour! The woman who makes 75 years look lit! I even tried to holla at her, but she told me I was too wet behind the ears!" We all laughed because that sounded just like something she'd say. "Everybody rise to your feet and give it up for the fierce and sexy MaryAnn Boyce, better known as MAAAAAAAAA-MMMMMAAAYYYYY!!!!"

We all erupted into cheer as two of my little cousins rolled out a red carpet and two others acted as security in their black pants and tees with the words "SECURITY" displayed across the front. The way they wore their dark shades and touched earpieces like they were talking to somebody made them even more adorable. Ma-May followed in a knee-length, A-line, gold glittery off the shoulder dress. She had on some gold, flat, strappy sandals, and gold accessories, looking amazing! Everyone cheered her on, and the photographers served as her paparazzi as she came dancing down the carpet to the dance floor. Once she made it to the dance floor, the DJ changed the song to the TikTok version and Ma-May's security started doing the challenge. After their turn, Ma-May joined in, doing the challenge and killing it! I just looked on in amazement, just praying that I look and act like this when I'm her age. We all eventually joined her on the dance floor, then we took a break for greeting and eating.

Zena and I took our turn through the buffet line and headed towards the tented area for a table. There were a few seats scattered and a pub table with no chairs, meant for standing only. We didn't mind leaving the seats for the older guests who were unable to stand. And worst-case scenario, we could either go sit in one of our cars or just go in the den. Just as we opened our to-go boxes, Eden waddled towards us with Remy in tow. Looking hot and miserable, she sat in one of the vacant seats by us.

"You okay, Sis?" I asked.

"Not hardly. My back is aching, and these shoes are too tight."

"My booty shaking from left to right!" Zena and I blurted at the same time and fell into a fit of laughter.

As miserable as she was, Eden couldn't hold her laughter, and Remy joined in once he realized it was safe to do.

Remy decided to go take a smoke break and promised he'd bring her back pillow when he returned. We decided to walk with him because Zena wanted to hit the blunt. Remy parked close to the edge of the property so that he would be able to slide out easily, if necessary. So, we posted up by his car, using the magnolia trees for shade. Usually, we played music, but the way the DJ's speakers were echoing through the neighborhood, there was no need.

Remy pulled out a bag from his glove box with three pre-rolled blunts and a lighter.

"Uh-uh Rem, I told you about bringing that pre-rolled shit around here. I don't know what's in that, and you not about to have me embarrassing myself in front of Ma-May and all these folks!"

"Girl, shut up." Remy replied while lighting up. "You know I rolled these myself. I knew it was gonna be a long day, so I came fully prepared. But your ass can go get your own. More for me."

Zena rolled her eyes and whispered, "That's all you had to say."

I chuckled at their exchange because they were my real life Craig and Day-Day. I didn't smoke with them, although I'd caught plenty contact highs in their presence. I had smoked in my past, but once Lucas expressed how much he didn't like women who smoked weed, I just left it alone. We began the smoke session with small talk about the party and how Ma-May was doing her big one, then Remy started expressing his nervousness about becoming a father and being there for Eden during this pregnancy. We made sure to reassure him that he's a great brother, cousin, and husband, and he would be even greater once the baby arrived...although he still hadn't taken Eden her pillow. It was all jokes because we knew Eden would've been on his ass if she needed it immediately.

Everything kinda settled into a peaceful silence as my thoughts drifted back to my BBQ Savior. I wondered if I would ever see him again or if he was just an angel to help me in my time of need. The way this man glowed, he was definitely giving Gabriel vibes. Zena pulled me from my thoughts when she stated, "Nih, look at this dude on the grill, cross the street. He has gotta be the only person on the block who is not at this party. And he looks like he's alone. That's some sad shit."

Remy and I both looked in the direction across from us, but I couldn't really see anything more than a silhouette. I guess the sun was blocking. Remy must have recognized him because he jumped up and ran across the street. We watched them dap each other up and began talking. After about ten minutes or so, Remy walked back towards the car, grabbing Eden's pillow, and let us know that was his coworker, and he would be joining us soon. We all headed back to rejoin the festivities. Everybody was surrounding the stage area doing the Cha-Cha slide, while Ma-May was actually on the stage leading the shenanigans.

As she saw us approaching, Ma-May screamed into the microphone, "There go my babies! Come on and dance with Ma-May! It's my birthday, Chile!"

As much as I despised that damn dance, I filed in, as did Zena. Remy went to check on Eden, so he was able to get out of it. The Cha Cha Slide turned into The Electric Slide, then The Cupid Shuffle, then The Biker Shuffle. I finally tapped out during K Wang Wit' It. I grabbed a cold water from the cooler and sat beside Zena on the yard swing like we used to do as kids. It was now after 6pm and the temperature was finally cooling down. A lot of the older guests had taken refuge inside of the barn, which was more suitable and comfortable for them. The younger cousins and guests were scattered about playing cards, dancing, and socializing. As we swung on the old swing, allowing the wind to caress my face, my mind went back to my grocery story superhero. So many questions plagued my mind. Why didn't he try to pursue me? Was I that damaged that it was starting to show on the outside? Of all the days to meet me, why one of my worst days?

As if she could read my thoughts, Zena asked, "Do you think you'll ever see him again?"

She and I were more than cousins. She was like my soul sister. We felt each other's energies, could finish each other's sentences, and just knew what we needed to be for one another at any given time. Knowing who she was referring to, I responded, "God, I hope so. But Z, I don't know if he would even want me. I'm an emotional hot mess."

"Kali, you're not a hot mess. You've had a traumatic experience. Lucas's bitch ass broke your heart and your spirit. And you're healing. Proper healing doesn't always feel good, and it takes time. Give yourself grace, Love. And when you do heal fully, you're going to wreck shit in the most beautiful way. But in the meantime, don't miss out on life grieving the death of that tired relationship y'all had."

We just looked at each other silently and fell back in the swing laughing. Zena couldn't stay serious for nothing. She made valid points but had to go left every time. As Remy made his way in our direction, we settled down a bit to observe his friend walking with him. He was introducing his friend to everyone along their path. Because the sun was shining so bright, I had shades on, but the silhouette of this man made me pull them down a bit.

"Damn, is that the neighbor?" Zena asked.

"Must be, but I must've been in the heat too long because he looks too familiar." I responded.

I recognized that tall, slender frame with the slightly bowlegged stride. He was dressed in khaki cargo shorts and a fitted white polo shirt, giving a slight imprint of his abs underneath. He wore some brown and khaki low top Clarks to match. He must've changed clothes because I thought I saw a t-shirt and basketball shorts earlier. As he got closer, I noticed the waves glistening in the sun like he just moisturized and brushed each strand to perfection. Couldn't be. Ain't no way. This had to be a mirage because, *what*?! They finally approached us, and I began studying his smooth skin, full lips, and big cognac-colored eyes. My body reacted to him immediately, and I felt the rapid increase in my heart rate and instant moistening in between my legs, confirming that this was, in fact, the nameless man on my mind.

Remy continued their round of introductions with, "And this is my sister and cousin that you saw me with earlier."

Before he could say anything else, Zena blurted out, "Yeah, I'm Zena. I'm the one who noticed you looking lonely as hell over there."

His sexy chuckle caused the pit of my stomach to drop like I was descending the peak of roller coaster. "Nice to meet you, Zena." He shook her hand. "Thanks for noticing. It was getting pretty awkward watching a whole block party unfold."

Then he turned to me with his hand outstretched and asked, "And you are?"

As if his aura commanded it, my right arm extended without my help. I managed to muster, "I'm Kalyani."

As our hands connected, his grin widened, as he stared into my soul. Then with a deep breath, he replied, "Nice to meet you, Kalyani. I'm Aeson."

6

AESON

As I was standing outside tending to my grill, I was peeping out my neighbor's party across the street. People were everywhere, and cars were still piling in. The smell from the grills combined with my grill had me so hungry, I was eating my food while it was entirely too hot, burning up my mouth. The DJ or emcee had the party rocking. The music echoed throughout the neighborhood so loudly that I just went ahead and turned mine off since I could barely hear it anyway. I knew that the neighborhood was very tight knit, but I hadn't really had the opportunity to meet a lot of my neighbors yet. I saw the lady across the street whenever she walked to get her newspaper in the mornings, but because I was always on my way to work, we only said our "Good mornings" and kept it moving. Now I wished I would have taken more time to get to know everybody so that I could be invited. Even though I was used to being by myself, this actually made me feel lonely.

As I was in my thoughts, I noticed Remy jogging across the street from the party towards me. "Rem, what's up, man? Whatchu doing on this side of town? I thought you lived in

Layton." We dapped each other's hands and gave a one shoulder hug. Lowkey, I was happy to see a familiar face.

"What up, Aes?!" I didn't realize you lived across the street from my grandmother. I would have made sure to invite you to her 75th birthday party."

"Mrs. MaryAnn is your grandmother? It's a small world, Bo." I replied.

"Yeah, that's my mom's mom. We call her Ma-May though. She swears she's too young to be a grandma, even though she's actually a great grandma," he said, chuckling and shaking his head.

"That's what's up. I've seen her a few times in the mornings. I would've never guessed she was seventy-five though. That's a blessing."

"Yeah, it is, and she made sure we celebrated it. You busy over here? You should come join us."

"Nah, it's just me. I wanted a little something to eat, so I got me a grill," I said swatting the grill with my hand towel for emphasis. " Y'all putting my lil' solo cookout to shame though. You sure she won't mind?" I really couldn't contain my eagerness to be around others for a change, but I would never intrude.

"Nah," Remy assure. "I promise it's cool."

"Ok, bet. Let me put my stuff up, clean up a bit, then I'll shoot you a text when I'm ready to head over."

"Ok, bet." We dapped each other up again and he jogged back across the yard. I noticed two ladies waiting on him, but I couldn't really get an unobstructed view because of the sun.

I took my food off the grill and put everything up in containers to eat later. Since I cleaned as I cooked, I did not have much to do in the kitchen. I wiped down my counters again, for added measure, then took a shower to change into something more presentable. Once I got dressed, I ran out to the nearby Walgreens to grab a birthday card and placed seventy-five dollars in it. I didn't feel right showing up empty handed, especially considering I wasn't technically invited in the first place. Once I arrived back, I shot Remy a text to let him know I was about to walk over.

He met me as I strode up the long driveway and stated, "You know you didn't have to get so spiffy. We're all family here. And did you go get a card, nigga?!"

I replied, "Bruh, I cannot go around these people dressed in basketball shorts and a tee. Gotta at least make a good first impression. And yes, I got her a card. It's her birthday."

"Yeah, a'ight, then. She'll appreciate it, for sure. Let me introduce you to her and a few guests. It's too many people to introduce everybody."

Remy walked me around and introduced me to many people, including his wife, a few other neighbors that I'd seen before, and some other relatives that I did not know. I shook hands and hugged several people, but a woman on the swing kept grabbing my attention. She was a little far away so I couldn't really see her too well, but it was as if her energy was pulling me. Before I could head in her direction or ask Remy about her, he nudged me in the direction of a beautiful older lady with short sisterlocs, so I followed his lead.

"Ma-May, this is your neighbor from across the street, Aeson. We actually work together so I invited him over once I realized he lived there."

"Happy birthday, Mrs. MaryAnn. It's a pleasure to formally meet you. And here's a little something for your big day." I extended the card out to her with a smile.

As she grabbed the card, she pulled me in for a tight hug and chattered, "Hey, baby! I'm so glad you could make it. I actually came by your house to invite you, but you weren't home. I was hoping you'd come over. We're all family in this neighborhood. Did you get something to eat?"

She rattled off so much so fast, I didn't know what to respond to first, so I answered, "Thank you for being so welcoming. I haven't eaten yet, but I will."

"Ok, baby. Well, enjoy yourself and don't call me MaryAnn no mo'. I'm Ma-May to you. Capiche?" She pointed her left index finger with her long, decorated nails and placed her right hand on her hip. Her eyes gave a no-nonsense stare like The Rock but was softened by the grin on her face. I could tell that her kids and grandkids probably knew that look all too well.

I laughed as Remy shrugged his shoulders and responded with, "Yes, ma'am."

Finally, we headed in the direction of the two women on the swing. As I got closer, her features became distinguishable.

No way this was *her*. Couldn't be. Was I trippin'? And did he say my damsel in distress was *his sister*? I had to tear my eyes away from her for just a moment to acknowledge their cousin, but once our eyes connected, I was locked in. Everyone could have disappeared in that moment. It was just her and me.

Kalyani.

This woman was so beautiful. I don't know if it was the sunlight beaming on her melanin or the good vibes, but she was glowing. A major contrast of the woman I helped in the grocery store. By the look on her face, she had to be in shock that it was me. I assume the expression on her face mimicked my inner emotions, but I tried to play it cool. What were the odds that her brother was my coworker, and her grandmother was my neighbor, directly across the street, at that. I do not believe in coincidences, so I was very intrigued at this point. Seeing her in this element was quite different from our earlier encounter.

She still had her hair the same as earlier, but she changed into some light denim shorts, a white crop top, and some brown sandals. A gold rope necklace decorated her neck, along with the same big hoop earrings she wore earlier. As she removed the shades from her eyes, I could see the entirety of her honey-brown irises, as her eyes widened in disbelief. Seeing her stuck made me smile a little, but I tried to keep it chill.

After exchanging names, Remy interrupted, suggesting that we head over to the buffet style spread. I nodded in agreement because I was hungry and wanted to catch him up on my earlier interaction with Kalyani. I couldn't see him behind me, but I'm sure he wondered what was going on between us. Zena didn't hide the look of confusion on her face, but she remained quiet and tuned in. I uttered to her softly, "I'm glad I got your name this time. It's beautiful, Kalyani."

She smiled and uttered, "Thank you, Aeson." I couldn't help but smile as I followed Remy's lead to the food.

Once we were a few feet away from the ladies, he asked, or rather stated, "So you know my sister, huh?"

And as if on cue, I heard Zena blurt out from behind us, "*BARBECUE BAE*?! Thaaaattt's Barbecue Bae?!"

Followed by Kalyani with, "Girl, shut your loud ass up!"

I couldn't help but laugh and answered his question. "Yeah, I actually met her this morning." I gave him the rundown of how I ran into her at the store, then I stated, "She seemed to be a little stressed out so I just wanted to help her out a bit. She looks like she's doing better though."

As the servers placed food on my plate, I noticed Remy stopped walking and just looked at me. "Why are you lookin' at me like that, Bo?"

"You're feeling my sister, ain't it?" he asked, smiling ear to ear.

I had to be mimicking his expression when I answered, "Yeeeaahhh, Bo."

We laughed loudly and finished piling our plates. There was so much food, I had to get two to-go boxes and still fought the urge to fix another one. My plates were to the brim with perloo, string beans, mac and cheese, baked beans, collard greens, pasta salad, hot dog, ribs, chicken, and pork chop. This was the type of meal I was missing. My spread would have sufficed, but it did not compare to this. And I hadn't even gotten any desserts yet.

As we traveled to a vacant table under one of the tents, I noticed Kalyani taking pictures with a group of ladies. There was a professional photographer and videographer walking around taking candids, while others had their phones out making memories. The huge smile on her face tugged at my heart, but it lost its grip as my heart melted hearing her laugh. Not one of those laughs to make you look cute. It was *genuine*.

Remy stuffed a fork full of beans in his mouth before stating, "Listen, me and Kali are close as hell. I've always looked out for her, but I had to let her be her own person and make her own choices. With that being said, she just got out of a relationship not even two months ago. I never liked that nigga because he wasn't good enough for her. Instead of leveling up to her, he brought her down to his level. It's like he was jealous of all she had, even though she was offering up the best of herself to him. She never really went into a lot of details about the things he did, but I do know he was cheating on her. Once she found out, she finally let him go." I listened to him in disbelief. Not that I didn't believe what he was saying, but I couldn't wrap my head around a nigga mistreating that alluring woman who captivated me even in her sadness. Remy continued, "I think you would be good for her though. She needs a real man in her life. You think you're up for the challenge?"

"I don't think it's really a challenge. It's about the vibe. Everybody has a story, but what's your next chapter? I'm a grown man, and I know what I want. And on some real shit, I want Kalyani. She caught my attention the moment I saw in her Publix, but I could tell she had some hurt she was dealing with. I don't want to intervene in someone's situation, and I also don't want to hinder anyone's healing journey, but there's just something about her, Bo."

Remy just stared at me for a moment before stating, "Damn, Bro. I didn't know you were this sensitive and shit. D'Angelo ass nigga."

I almost spit my lemonade out laughing so hard.

"For real though, want me to talk you up to her?"

"I appreciate that man, but nah. If it's cool with you, I'm gonna go holla at her. But I can't on an empty stomach. I hongry, Bo! This shit bussin'!"

Remy shook his head and laughed. He always found it funny when my accent made an appearance. "That's wassup. If I can give you any advice, just be patient with her."

"I feel you." And with that, we changed the subject and continued eating our food. I wanted to watch her vibe out a little more before I made any moves.

7

KALYANI

"**B**ih! First of all, you didn't tell me that man was *that* damn fine. No wonder your mood changed. What are the odds that your Barbecue Bae is Remy's coworker AND Ma-May's neighbor? This is some divine intervention for your ass. Even God say he tired of you worrying behind Lucas and his bullshit."

"Z, you get on my nerves, but you might be right," I replied while low key watching Aeson eat and interact with Remy. I don't know what they were cracking up about, but I was jealous that I wasn't a part of the conversation. His smile was so captivating, and his laugh was so sultry, even his laugh lines were sexy. I tried to give them their space and mind my business, but I was so drawn to this man. I couldn't help it.

"Kali, why won't you just go talk to him? He looks like he's just as interested in you as you are in him."

"You think so? I mean, I thought I felt something, but I don't want to embarrass myself."

"Babygirl, you keep forgetting who the hell you are. You are *that* girl!"

"But what if he doesn't see that I'm 'that girl?' Luke didn't recognize it. I don't even know if she's still in me. I'm just - I can't take getting any more broken than I am already. And we don't even know if this man is single or not."

"But what if he *is* single, Kali? And what if he *does* see it? Because the look in that man's eyes says he saw it." Zena spoke as she looked directly into my eyes. "Cousin, **Eff** Lucas!" Still trying not to curse around her elders. "And nobody is telling you to marry the man. Just talk to him. Have fun. You know the best way to get over one man is to get under another one." Then she shoulder-bumped me for emphasis.

"I swear I can never take you seriously," I said while rolling my eyes.

"But you know I'm right, tho! That man came over here glistening like he just rubbed on the heavenliest oils, that frankincense and mirth. And doesn't his neck look sturdy?"

"Sturdy?! What are you even talking about?"

"Sturdy! Like thick and strong."

I eyed her with the utmost confusion.

"See this is why you need some. That man's neck is strong enough to bear the weight of arms and thighs!"

"Girl, shet uuupppp!" She was looking so serious while I was bursting at the seams laughing. This was our dynamic. She would say something off the wall while I laughed at her shenanigans.

"You can laugh all you want to, but you need to go talk to that man. You're lucky I like 'em light and bright. I'd be all in his face right now, making him want to taste me instead of that food."

And with that, I abruptly stopped laughing. She hit a nerve, and she knew it. Her hypothetical scenario had me jealous as hell. *How did this man have me like this?* "I'm gonna talk to him. Just not right now." Changing the subject and shifting her attention to our cousins nearby pulling out their phones and selfie sticks, I said, "Come on, let's go take pics!" Reluctantly, she agreed. Aeson and

I would have our time. Just not now. I had to get my thoughts together first.

We spent the next hour or so taking pictures, dancing, and socializing, while Ma-May had the time of her life. Intermittently, I stole glimpses of Aeson, and I even caught him glaring back at me a few times. In the midst of all the commotion going on around me, I found myself in solitude mentally, mulling over whether I should take the chance to talk to him. I felt like my conscience sat the opposing forces on my shoulders and they were pleading their case. But instead of an angel and devil, it was the fearless tigress and the scaredy cat. On one hand, I was too fresh out of a relationship. Even though I was emotionally disconnected from Lucas long before I got the nerve to end things, there was so much damage already done, and I didn't know if it was reparable. The verbal and emotional abuse brought me to a place where I didn't even recognize myself anymore. I knew I was beautiful. I knew I was smart. I knew that not only did I bring a lot to the table, but I could also multiply it and make it better. My heart was genuine, and I loved hard. But that was also my downfall. He took my kindness and manipulated it until it became my weakness. Lowering my defenses, he broke me with his words and his actions. Now here I was trying to build myself back up. So there lies the question: Was I even ready to indulge in a situation with someone else? Could I handle it? I was a romantic - a lover of love - and look where I ended up. Was I too fragile?

That's where the opposing side stepped up, sounding a lot like Zena, saying, "Hell yeah, you can handle it!" I deserved my desired happiness even if it wasn't forever. To find love, you had to take chances and never lose hope. And a connection this strong demanded exploration. Even if it was just a physical one. That alone was worth exploring. And if it didn't lead to anything, at least I would know.

The tigress won the debate, so I was waiting on the courage

and the opportunity to shoot my shot. I wasn't really a drinker, and Ma-May didn't want any hard liquor at her party because she said she was not about to deal with any drunkards on her birthday. But there was wine, which was enough for me. A couple glasses of Stella would get me together. I just had to keep my mind in check, with the understanding that we would be exploring possibilities. That's it!

As I came back to reality, I noticed that I had separated myself from the group, undoubtedly looking crazy in a daze. Regaining focus, I noticed that the sun was setting and the décor lightening was more prominent, intimately illuminating the area. I scanned the scene around me, and to my right, my teen cousins were teaching my older cousins TikTok dances. To the left, there was Aeson waltzing in my direction. Did I summons this man in my mind?

"Hey, Kalyani. Are you ok?" he asked with a tilted head and furrowed brow, as if concerned for my wellbeing. Damn, his concern was so sexy.

"Yeah, I'm good. Thank you." I chuckled, and he visibly exhaled in relief. "I was just in deep thought about something."

"Ok, cool. Wanna talk about it? Ya know, since I wanted to talk to you alone anyway." His voice was so deep and sensual, never breaking eye contact. And his eyes emanated a spark that had me fixated.

"Uh... sure. Is the swing okay?" I inquired.

"The one y'all were bogarting earlier? Yeah, we can."

I laughed as he placed his hand at the small of my back, allowing me to lead the way. Once I sat down, he situated himself to the left of me, close enough for conversation, but still giving a respectful amount of room in between us. The swing wasn't huge, but there was space since our thighs were not touching.

We sat quietly for a moment, and though I gazed around in nervousness, I felt his eyes piercing me intently. I broke the silence by saying, "I'm sure you weren't expecting to see the stressed out chick from Publix again. Small world, right?"

Aeson leaned forward, rubbing his hands down his thighs, then rested his elbows there, never breaking his stare. Then he stated reassuringly, "Yeah, it was unexpected, but I'm grateful. And even more, seeing the smile that's been plastered on your face since I got here." A smile graced his face, causing me to smile like Justice when Lucky kissed her in the hair salon. And this man hadn't even touched me yet! My cheeks felt like they were on fire from blushing so hard. Aeson had me so hot, I wanted to melt. I couldn't even formulate a sentence after that.

He continued with, "And it is a small town in a small world, but I don't believe in coincidence. I genuinely believe that everything happens for a reason. Meeting you this morning, your brother being the only coworker I really vibe with, and your grandmother across the street was God's divine intention."

I found my voice, replying, "I agree. There is something here, but I'm just getting out of a relationship and not ready to jump into anything right now."

"It was evident earlier that you were dealing with a situation, which is why I didn't pursue you then. But seeing you again, I'm not about pass up this opportunity. Now, I'm not implying anything by saying this, but I would like to get to know you better and find out our purpose."

The more Aeson talked, the more comfortable and confident I felt. Even after meeting me at my worst, he felt there was *something* within me worth pursuing. Maybe Zena was right.

Just as the thought entered my mind, her silly ass walked by grinning and waving like she was a little kid. "Hey, y'all. Ain't y'all cute!" And with the quickness, we saw a white flash and her hauling ass away from us.

"Please excuse Zena. That girl has no chill and even less filter."

"It's cool. I like her vibe. I can tell she's Ma-May's grandchild."

"Lawddd, she already has you calling her Ma-May?! I hope you know you have now been recruited as a grandchild."

Aeson cleared his throat before responding. "I'm cool with that. It's appreciated."

His eyes appeared to gloss over a bit, making me wonder what he meant by that, but since we had just established this friendship or whatever, I didn't want to pry or make him regret it. Changing the subject I asked, "Wassup with the accent? Where are you from?"

Teasingly, he joked, "What accent? I sound like you, innit?"

"Hell no, you don't!" I replied quickly, and we both laughed.

"Nah, I've only been in Bay Springs a couple months. I'm from Maxton, but my parents were from the low country of South Carolina. They moved right after they got married, but I picked up on some of the dialect from living with them."

Before I could ask any more questions, the DJ played Fantasia's "When I See You," and guests headed to the dance floor. I began dancing in my seat to the intro, eyes closed and all. Opening them, I heard Aeson say, "Oh, that's my shit right there." With his hand outstretched, he commanded, "Come dance with me." And we made our way to join the others.

8

AESON

I heard Remy yell, "Yo DJ! Run that back!" as he and Eden
made their way to the floor as well. Fantasia really did her
big one with this song because it was one of my favorites, and
probably my most favorite cut by a female artist. Dancing with
Kalyani made me love it even more. There were quite a few
people dancing around us, but they all faded away as I watched
her lip sync the lyrics with her eyes on mine. I can tell it was
getting good to her when she closed her eyes and sang loudly
and off pitch. And I joined in and made it a duet, and we cut up
like we were doing a remake of the video.

"Something now is taking overrrrrr meeeeeeee!!! Ye-ye-ye-ye-ye-yeahhh!!"

Her vibe was intoxicating. It's not easy to find someone whom
you can match energies so effortlessly. Her laugh was just as
equally adorable as her wide smile that caused her nose to upturn
slightly. This girl was fine. We two-stepped and sang to each
other through a few more songs. The DJ must have felt the vibes
because he was on point.

As "Anything" by Jaheim began to play, I pulled Kalyani close to me, wrapping my arms around her waist while hers enclosed around my neck. Our sways synchronized as she relaxed her body into mine. Though I towered over her, I could still feel her heart beating until the two combined fell into a cadence. Her eyes seemed to search mine as I mumbled the words. It didn't hurt that I could hold a tune. "Aesonnnn..." she stated as her eyes widened then narrowed slightly at the revelation, and I smiled and continued to sing to her. Not many people knew about my little gift besides my immediate family. It was a gift that I chose to keep to myself. If I happened to be singing absentmindedly and someone heard me, I stopped. It wasn't that I was shy; I just didn't feel like I was supposed to share my gift with everyone. She shifted her focus from my eyes down to my lips, inflicting her to bite her own. As if I could read her mind, I gently pressed my lips to her forehead. Kalyani embraced me tightly, wrapping her arms around my waist, placing her hands on my back and resting her head on my chest. Anthony Hamilton's "Change Your World" blared through the speakers as if my mom was giving me her approval.

In one day, Kalyani had managed to change my world. For the first time in my life, I felt no reservations. This felt *right*, and I had to have her. Figuring out when and how to tell her without her thinking I was crazy was the hard part. Did she even feel the same about me? Was she even ready to be in a relationship, considering her recent breakup? The last thing I wanted to do was force her into something she wasn't ready for and ultimately ending up pushing her away. Even if she wasn't ready, I'd wait on her. That's how sure I was that this was *my wife*. But I knew that my level of assertion could intimidate her, so I had to handle her with care. She was worth it.

Breaking us out of our trance, the DJ lowered the music, asking everyone inside the building to come out and for Ma-May to come front and center. As she stood there, undoubtedly knowing what was coming, two women came down the aisle with a rolling cart that held a huge cake with sparkler candles. The DJ began the newly popular TikTok birthday song, and we all joined in. Once she blew out her candles, fireworks began to light up the sky. Either the neighbors had impeccable timing or the family really went all out for her birthday. The caterers were passing out cake slices as guests enjoyed the fireworks show.

"Would you like to have a seat?" I asked.

"Yeah, let's go back to the swing so I can eat my cake." She replied.

As we turned to mosey in that direction, I stated, "I'm sure somebody's already sitting there by now."

She stopped to look at me and firmly stated, "And I'm sure they're gonna get their ass up too."

I just laughed at her country hood ass and let her lead the way.

As we approached, Zena stood up with a big grin on her face, saying, "Don't worry, Cuzzy. I got y'all covered," and walked away.

I must've had a shocked look on my face because Kalyani simply stated, "Told ya," and stuffed cake in her mouth.

"Yoooooo, how you mean y'all Debo them people outchea! You fool up!" I said, laughing.

She just looked at me with a closed-mouth smile and asked, "What the hell you say?!"

I broke it down for her. "How are y'all gonna tell somebody they can't sit here? Y'all crazy."

Kalyani just gave a soft giggle and leaned back as we swung and watched the show. After a few moments, she broke the silence by stating, "I'm glad I met you. And I'm so glad you're here."

"Me too," I replied. I wanted to say so much more, but I needed to gauge her mind frame a little more.

"I've been through a lot, Aeson. My last situation hurt me. He broke me. But there is something about you. I don't know what it is, but I feel you. Like I literally *feel* you. Just be patient with me."

Before I could respond, Zena came power walking over with a sense of emergency. You could tell she was trying not to cause a scene, but it was urgent. I stood up in protective mode and Kalyani stood behind me. "What's wrong, Z?"

"Girl, Remy about to beat that nigga's ass. Come on!"

Kalyani's eyes widened as her mouth dropped, while I replied, "The fuck?!"

I didn't know what was going on, but Remy was my boy, and I had his back. We quickly marched towards the long driveway, where the cars were parked, to see Remy and some guy arguing. A couple guys I was introduced to as cousins were holding Remy back, while an older male stood in between the men. From a distance, it looked like a group of guys chillin', mindfully not causing a disturbance out of respect. Remy stood slightly shorter than my 6'2" frame, at 6'0" maybe, but we were about the same medium build. I recognized the older male in the middle to be his father that I met earlier, Mr. Jamison. He and Remy were practically *copy and paste* of each other, except Remy was slightly slimmer and hair wasn't gray yet.

The other dude was shorter, maybe 5'9" or 5'10" and kinda built. There was a tall, slim dude with him who was trying to convince him to leave.

"Yo, I asked you to leave so leave! Why the fuck you still here?! Get the fuck on, bruh," Remy roared.

"Lucas, it's Ma-May's birthday. This is not the time or the place," Mr. Jamison added.

"I know. I wasn't trying to cause no problems. I had Ma-May's gift and wanted to bring it by and hopefully talk to Kali. That's it," the nigga I learned as Lucas pleaded.

"She don't wanna see your bitch ass and you weren't invited, so get the fuck on." Remy interjected.

This was Kalyani's ex?! Did she know he was coming? In the short time I'd known him, I'd never seen him so upset. And I was surprised when Mr. Jamison replied, "I'll take your gift. Say your peace then leave. I got shit to do." He turned to Kalyani saying, "Just listen to his ass so Remy doesn't cause a scene. I don't wanna hear the women's mouths up there."

"Ok, Daddy," she agreed.

She looked at me with pleading eyes, and I asked, "You sure?"

"Yeah, I'm ok."

So I stepped back and let her handle her business. A part of me wanted to leave her alone and let her deal with her shit, but I couldn't get the urge to. Remy came over to me, to give them a little room. "I don't like this shit, Aes."

"Me either, Rem. But just give her this moment. She knows we got her back." I glanced over at Zena, and she looked like she was ready to pounce at any given moment. What have I gotten myself into?

9

KALYANI

I couldn't believe this. My day was going entirely too well. Considering how my day started off, life took a whole 180-degree turn meeting Aeson. I felt so comfortable with him after the initial shock wore off. Plus, this man was so fine, I could just stare at him all day and be okay with doing that and nothing else. Dancing with him was pure heaven. He held on to me so firmly, yet gentle at the same time, and he smelled so damn good. He was wearing some variation of Azzaro, if I had to guess, but I made a mental note of finding out which one because he was getting a whole gift basket full of it. Our rhythms fell in sync so naturally, and when he sang in my ear, the hairs on my neck stood on end. I felt like I could've come on myself at that very moment. And I could see his desire for me in his eyes. He wanted me just as badly as I wanted him. He was the perfect distraction from my problems.

Then Lucas's dumb ass showed up. This man was relentless. Why would you show up to my grandmother's birthday party after we broke up? It wasn't like this was an amicable breakup. I couldn't stand his narcissistic ass. And my daddy. I wish I could say that I couldn't believe him either, but that was the norm for him. I loved my daddy dearly, but he didn't care much if it didn't affect him personally. Remy, on the other hand, always supported and protected me. So much in fact, all his childhood fights were because of some kid bothering me, whether it was a school bully or one of our cousins. So, it was nothing for him to beat Lucas's ass, especially since he knew all the details of our relationship. Respect for Ma-May saved his ass today.

My dad suggested I talk to Lucas, and although I hated the idea of even listening to his voice, maybe it was necessary for me to move on. And if not, hopefully, it would at least get him to leave without causing a scene, getting his ass whooped. Aeson stood in front of me like my own personal bodyguard, while he watched this bullshit unfold. This was so embarrassing, considering the great time we were having. How ironic that the moment I opt to tell Aeson about what I had been through, this nigga showed up. He said he would be patient with me, and God wasted no time setting up the stage. This moment would surely be a test of his patience.

I stepped from behind Aeson, walking in front of him and Remy. Although it was dark out, the driveway was lit with various lighting, allowing me to notice Lucas's eyes shift from Remy to Aeson with a confused expression.

"What do you want Lucas?" I asked with a blank stare.

Eyes still shifting, he spoke in a low tone, asking, "Can we talk in private?"

We stepped a few more feet away from everyone, but I knew they were ear hustling, waiting to see what happens. My back was to them, but they could see Lucas's face clearly.

Once we stopped, I crossed my arms across my chest and inquired, "What do you want?"

"I miss you, Kay," he replied with a slight grin, using his right hand to graze my upper left arm.

I jerked my shoulder away from his touch and warned in a low tone, "Keep your fuckin' hands off me." I didn't want to get too loud, knowing that The Goon Squad was right behind me. I could tell he was thinking the same thing from the way he looked back in their direction.

"Why you actin' like this? Like you don't miss a nigga? It's time to cut the bullshit, yo. Real shit."

Lucas and I met almost six years ago when he came into the bank, where I was a teller. He came in quite often, so we always found something to talk or joke about. He was very attractive to me: handsome, funny, educated, a business owner, financially stable, and no children. He seemed perfect, but I had a thing about dating customers…I didn't. Customers were completely off limits to me. After a few months, I ran into him while grabbing takeout. He struck up a conversation while waiting on our food, and he ended up asking for my number. Against my better judgment, I decided to give him a chance. Things were great in the beginning. Lucas catered to me and spoiled me with gifts and trips without me even asking. Even though my family loved him, Remy remained cordial but kept him at arm's length. He made sure not to get too close to him. He told me that as long as I was happy, he was happy, but the moment I wasn't, all bets were off with him and Lucas. After a couple of years, Lucas slowly started changing and trying to change me. He no longer wanted to go out with me or go on trips but complained when I did things without him. My clothes soon became an issue. They were either too tight, too short, or too revealing, including clothes he bought for me. I wasn't by any means a skinny girl, but I was always rather fit. I dressed in form fitting clothes but never anything too revealing or too short. I frequented the gym so much that gym attire was my main after work wardrobe, and he would accuse me of flirting, enticing, or sleeping with the guys there.

From there, the relationship only got worse with the verbal

and psychological abuse. He started berating me, calling me dumb and fat and started constantly telling me how nobody else would want to be with me because I didn't listen. Any little mistake I made resorted in the name calling, and eventually, I felt worthless and dumb, just like he said. In the beginning of our relationship, I made the mistake of entrusting him with personal feelings and situations, including the rocky relationship with my parents. In his efforts to break me, he insinuated how they didn't really care about me and that I had nobody. It didn't help that they adored him so much, like they favored him over me. I started secluding myself as I sank into a deep depression. I didn't want to tell anyone what I was dealing with because my parents would fault me for it, and I didn't want to look like an idiot to Remy and Zena. I mean, this was embarrassing. And I didn't want Remy to go to jail or get hurt behind my drama. I tried to leave a few times, but he knew what to say to convince me to stay.

A couple months ago, I finally got the courage to leave his ass for good. My family had a Memorial Day cookout here at Ma-May's house. I thought everything was fine until we were headed back to my townhouse. He started arguing about how I ignored him all day. For most of the day, the guys were outside under the tent playing cards while the ladies were inside the rec room. I came out a few times to bring him his food and check on him, so I didn't see where the problem was. Once we got back to my place, he followed me inside, still fussing. I'd had enough at this point, so I asked him to leave and told him I was done. That infuriated him to the point of raising his hand to hit me. At that point, I just yelled, "Alexa, call Remy!" This was my first time seeing him since he ran out my door. Scared. Like a bitch.

The next day, I received a DM from some random chick on Instagram named WorldzFinest27. She wasn't a new follower, but

I didn't recognize her to say I knew her personally. The message stated:

Hey Kalyani. I know you don't know me, but I've been with Lucas for the past year. He came to my house last night and beat my ass. I assume this was because of you. Can you please tell me what happened yesterday?

The audacity. And no, I didn't reply to her ass either.

Snapping back to reality, I replied, "Lucas, I don't know why you even thought there was a speck of a possibility of us getting back together. You put me down and degraded me for years for absolutely no reason. I was good to you! But the day you raised your hand to me, I was through. Hell, I was through before that, but now I'm THROUGH through. Then you got your lil' side bitch following me on IG on some stalker shit. Aaannnnddddd... you beat her ass when you couldn't mine?!"

I could tell he was getting upset as his nostrils flared. He just laughed a little and said, "Man, that bitch lying. And you know you wanna come back to me. Who the fuck else gonna want your slow ass? You said it yourself... nobody ever treated you as good as I did. And it would've kept going if you acted like you had some damn sense. You lucky I'm even willing to give you another chance! Dumb ass."

I zoned out and cursed him out with every fiber of my being, forgetting everything and everyone around me. He must have forgotten about them too because before he could lunge at me, Aeson grabbed me by my right arm and stood in front of me. Remy stood right beside him, and Zena was asking if I was ok. I didn't even know if I had the answer to that question.

Aeson spoke in a very calm voice, yet it was a little grittier than the voice I heard earlier. "Aye Boi. Go ahead before my bro box you up, my nigga."

"Yeah, nigga. I'm trying like hell to hold off on whooping

your ass," Remy stated. He had his hands in his pockets, trying to keep it together.

Lucas asked Aeson, "Bruh, this ain't got shit to do with you. I don't even know you. This between me and my lady, man."

"Looka hea, you don't need to know me. But I know I heard Babygirl say she ain't want nun to do witchu', innit?" The Geechie was coming out of him heavily, but it sounded so sexy.

"That's what the fuck I heard," Remy confirmed.

Lucas's homeboy seemed to appear from out of nowhere, considering how quiet he was through all of this. "Yo, I didn't come here for this shit, Luke. Let's go. This shit ain't cool, bruh."

"Listen to your people, man. We too old for this shit, but we can take it there," confirmed Remy.

"Fuck this shit," Lucas said as he retreated to his car. His friend was already a few steps ahead of him.

The guys turned towards me, and Remy came to hug me and asked, "Are you okay, Sis?" I nodded *yes* and gave him a partial smile.

Aeson hugged me next and whispered in my ear, "Are you sure you're okay? It's cool if you're not. No one is expecting you to be." With that, I exhaled and cried in his arms, releasing my brokenness with every tear. I had only ever felt truly safe with Remy around, and in one day, Aeson had given me safety, protection, and a sense of peace that I'd never experienced before. This man was too perfect.

10

AESON

I held Kalyani in my arms, giving her a moment to release all the emotions she was withholding. I remained silent, leaving her with her emotions, thoughts, and prayers, while rubbing her back and kissing her forehead ever so often. Remy and Zena had already walked back towards the house. In our silence, I began reflecting over the evening with my main question being, "How did we get here?" My plans for the day were to grill a little food and chill for the rest of the weekend. I never imagined that I'd meet a girl, meet her again, and vibe so well that I would be ready to beat her old dude's ass. But I don't regret a minute of it. I couldn't deny my attraction to Kalyani if I tried. I can't believe he actually came to the party. This dude had some big balls to be on that kinda time. Unfortunately, his homeboy wasn't on the same shit he was on. That dude didn't want no smoke. Lil buddy was asking for it though.

Although I barely knew the details of their previous relationship, I could tell that it took a major toll on Kalyani's life. Hell, I could tell that by the introduction at the grocery store. So, needless to say, I was baffled by her dad suggesting they talk. He either didn't read the room or didn't give a damn. I wanted to protest it myself, but I had to let it all play out. Plus, I had to keep my eyes on Remy while Zena tried to keep him calm. Everything was cool until I noticed her body language shifting from defensively crossing her arms to her arms flailing around and her voice getting louder as she yelled. When he touched her arm, I wanted to break his shit, but when he started disrespecting her, I knew he lost his damn mind. Dude was so mad, he forgot we were standing there. Had it not been Ma-May's party, I would've folded his ass, not to mention what Remy would've done. Lucky for him, common sense crept back in, and he left. But I could only hope that this incident wouldn't cause Kalyani to regress.

From the short distance, we could hear Ma-May on the microphone thanking everyone for taking time away from their 4th of July to celebrate her. We headed back towards the stage area, as she ran down her list of thanks and bid everyone good night by ending with the classic, "You don't have to go home, but you gotta get the hell outta here." A clean-up crew appeared out of nowhere and got to work. Kalyani decided to go help her family, and I went to assist Remy and his folks with folding tables and chairs.

"Y'all looking real cozy to say y'all just met today, Bruh! Iono how I feel about that," Remy said with a straight face.

"I don't know what to tell you, my boi. I wasn't expecting today to be like this, but I'm really feeling her. Like, *literally*, this energy is kinetic. This shit is crazy, but I'm wit all the shits. And anxious as hell to see where it leads."

Remy studied me a little longer with a straight face before breaking into a big ass grin, "Bruh, you gonna be my bro for real! This shit crazy!"

I laughed and told him, "Chill out, man. You were just bucking up at ol' boy and now you skinning and grinning!"

"Hell, yeah. For real tho, I appreciate you having my back.

And hers. It's always been me and Kali or me, Zena, and Kali. She trusts you, and you made her feel safe enough to do so. That's more than our own pops ever did. For that, I got your back always. Real shit." We dapped each other up and finished folding the tables and chairs.

11

KALYANI

After cleaning and fixing to-go plates, majority of the guests had left, while a few of the grandchildren still hung around. Zena and I decided to spend the night, and I assumed Remy and Eden were going to do the same, considering how she had already showered and was in bed. Ma-May had six bedrooms, so there was plenty of room. Zena and I had also taken our showers, blew up the air mattress in the den, and were watching *Living Single* reruns. Even as kids, we always chose to sleep on the floor in the den, but now that we were older, our backs couldn't handle that hard floor anymore. The king size air mattress fixed that issue. After awhile, I went into the kitchen to fix a bowl of vanilla ice cream with a slice of birthday cake, peeking out the window to see what the guys were doing. Remy, Aeson, and my twin cousins, PJ and DJ, were on the patio smoking blunts. A part of me wanted to pull Aeson to the side so that I could have his undivided attention, but the other part of me was too embarrassed to say anything at all. He must have thought I was crazy and too full of drama by now. And though he was extremely sweet and caring during my moment, I was sure he wanted to renege on his proposition to explore our purpose. I couldn't say anything, but that did not stop me from stalking through the blinds.

"What the hell you doing?!" Zena hollered , scaring the pure shit out of me.

"Girl! Stop playing so much! You gonna make me piss on myself!"

"Well, why are you stalking that man? You look like a creep."

"I wasn't stalking anybody. I looked out the damn window to see what the guys were doing. It was only for a quick second. You so extra," I walked out the kitchen, back into the den.

She followed right on my tail, saying, "Lies. I stood there for three minutes and fifty-two seconds before I said scared you. You were staring and stalking just like Joe from that show "You."" She plopped down on the air mattress while I sat on the floor Indian style as I finished my food. I didn't want to spill anything because technically, I wasn't supposed to be eating in the den anyway.

"You are so stuuuuupid," I laughed. "I didn't realize it was that long."

"Tuh," she said, rolling her eyes. "So, explain this to me. You meet this man early this morning, can't stop thinking about him, you find out he lives across the street, and is friends with your damn brother, thennnnnnnnn when he comes over, y'all get so boo'd up that you forget all about me, leaving me to talk to your cousins!! Now after the man defends your honor and consoles you when that rusty butt nigga tried it, you want to ignore him while he sits outside well after the party is over but stalk him through the blinds? I don't get it."

"Zena," I huffed with pleading eyes, "Please leave it alone."

"No!" she yelled at me, causing me to drop my spoon. "Why are you avoiding that man?! Yet you entertained Lucas with no fuckin' problem!"

"Why can't you mind your fuckin' business?!" I shouted back.

Before either of us could say another word, Ma-May came stomping into the den with her robe and bonnet on. "What the hell are y'all fussing about and why are you eating in my den?"

"My bad, Ma-May," I discarded my half-eaten plate in the trash. The conversation took away my appetite anyway. As I walked back towards them, I could hear Zena giving Ma-May the tea.

"And they look so good together, Ma, but she's running from him," I caught her saying.

Ma-May looked at me and ordered, "Sit down. Let's talk." I sat on the couch beside her while Zena remained on the air mattress. As we faced each other, she grabbed my hands and said, "Talk to me, Baby. What's wrong?" This was her classic move to get us to express our feelings. Something about this move made you want to bear your soul to her. And that's what I did. I busted into tears, while she hugged me tightly. I felt Zena rubbing my legs, attempting to console me as well. When I was finally able to speak, I explained why I didn't want to talk to Aeson.

"Ma, what do I have to offer that man? I am so broken. On day one, he's had to come to my rescue twice. That's not normal, and it's not fair to him. He's such a good man. I can tell that already. But he's too good for me. And Lucas reminded me that I'm not good enough. I wasn't good enough for *him*. I wasn't good enough for *my parents*. Why would I be good enough for Aeson?"

By this point, tears were streaming down all of our faces. I hated to bring other people down with me, but I also felt relief being able to release within the presence of loved ones who didn't mind helping me carry this burden.

Ma-May wiped my tears and affirmed, "Baby, you have so much to offer that man. Or any man. You are so beautiful with the sweetest spirit. You're so intelligent and successful. You're giving and you're strong. And if a man can't see that, it's because he's not meant to see it."

"What you mean?! I don't feel strong, Ma. I feel so weak. All I do is cry and hurt, and as soon as I start to feel better, I'm knocked back down," I contested.

Ma-May replied, "I hate what Lucas did to you, Kali. You overcame so much just to fall for a nigga who couldn't appreciate who he had. But God made you so much stronger than the hurt you experienced. And let me tell you something. Do not *ever* let anyone devalue you or make you question your self-worth. Everyone isn't going to recognize your merit, even when you're right in front of them. Some will see it and not know how to handle it with care. But there is going to be someone who sees it, recognizes it, appreciates it, and takes good care of it. Everybody can't spot a true diamond. You gotta have an eye for it, Baby."

"Aeson's fine ass got the eye, Ma-May. He fasho got it!" Zena always had a way of making us laugh. And with that being said, the mood was lightened and Ma-May began discussing her party. After another hour or so, the guys came inside and began fixing plates.

Ma-May fussed. "Don't come in here eating all the food after y'all done got all high up! Got my kitchen smelling like reefer. And Aeson, I'm disappointed in you. Don't let these boys corrupt you, nih!"

With a fake look of shame, Aeson replied, "Yes ma'am," and we all started laughing.

Ma-May hugged and kissed each one of us as she said, "I'm going to bed. Y'all better be up for breakfast in the morning. You too, Aeson!" When she got to me, she whispered in my ear, "Go talk to him. Now."

As if he heard her himself, Aeson walked over to me and stated, "It's getting kinda late, so I'm about to head out. Can I talk to you real quick before I go?"

I tried to mask my nervousness with a joke. "Oh, word? I thought you boys were having a sleepover."

He looked at me with low eyes and licked his lips, "Nah, the temptation would've been too strong. Ma-May would kick me outta here." My breath must've gotten caught in my throat because I didn't exhale until he grabbed my hand and said, "Let's go to the patio."

The aroma from the guys' smoke session still inhabited the covered patio. It was furnished with a sectional and a two more matching chairs, so we opted for the sectional. I sat first, and he followed, sitting close on my left with his right arm around me, resting on the back of the couch. As if I couldn't control my own body, I melted into his frame. And for a moment, we just sat in a peaceful silence. It was relatively dark, aside from the few lights decorating the yard and the light pole that lit in the close distance. The ceiling fan's brisk air combined with the night's lingering heat offered a balance of comfort and tranquility. I could feel him. His strong presence was all consuming. To think just moments earlier, I questioned whether I was good enough for him. At this particular moment, I felt his desire for me. To protect me and to care for me. How could I feel all this? Even more importantly, I had to ask myself, "Can you even handle a man like this?"

"So you avoiding me now?" Aeson asked, breaking our silence and pulling me from my thoughts.

"Huh?" Despite all my inner questions, I couldn't think of anything better to say.

"If you can 'huh,' you can hear." He quipped.

With that, I had to sit up and look at him, and he just stared me down with the utmost seriousness. We stayed in that position for a few moments, like he was challenging me to a duel of who could outstare who the longest. Then, I cracked, and we both fell out laughing.

"Bruh. Did you really just say that to me?" I implored, still highly amused at his ability to change my mood so effortlessly.

"I did. I figured if you didn't want to talk to me, I could at least get you to laugh with me."

And just like that, I leaned back into my rightful place, with his arm around me. I inhaled deeply and decided to lay my cards on the table, as his embrace gave me the ease I needed to tell him how I felt.

"Aeson, I'm sure you can tell that I'm really into you. This connection we have is so strong and weird and exciting and petrifying. I never felt this way about anybody before. I don't understand it, but I want it. I just don't know if I'm ready for it... mentally or emotionally."

"Why, because of that fuck nigga that was here earlier?" Aeson challenged. "What happened with that?"

I took a deep sigh and relayed, "Yes, because of him. I would love to tell you what happened, because I feel like I can confide in you. But honestly, it's exhausting and depressing. Right now, I just want to enjoy this peace with you."

"You want to enjoy this peace with me, but you hid from me for the past couple hours?" he accused, truly confused by my responses.

"I wasn't hiding. I just kept my distance. That shit was embarrassing! And I know you gotta be tired of saving me."

"Saving you?! Kalyani, I helped you with groceries. I had your back when that nigga tried to disrespect you. That's not saving you. That's *supporting* you. Babygirl, that's basic shit that any woman deserves." He lifted my chin as he continued to speak. "You deserve that level of care from a grown ass man. Not just your brother. Shiiitt, today barely scratches the surface of all I can and *will* be for you."

I felt the tears began to form but managed to keep them at bay. "Look, I know I'm broken. I have a lot of things to work on to repair what I allowed him to break, but I'm working on it. And it may seem contradictory, but as I heal from this, I still want to see how our friendship develops. Is that selfish?"

"Yes. It's selfish as hell. But who said selfish is a bad thing? You're telling me that you want to heal so you can be the best version of yourself when you become my woman, right?"

"That is not what I said," I replied, laughing.

"Well, that's what I heard. So, it is what it is. Nah mean?" he spoke in a lower, softer tone while appearing to study my face.

I closed my eyes, took another deep breath, and squeezed my thighs together tightly. That man's gaze alone sent my body into a frenzy, and I didn't know what to do. This was clearly a battle of my mind's telling me *no*, but my body was definitely telling me *hell yes*. And as my head nodded, it told him the same. And with that, Aeson leaned into me and placed his soft lips against mine, and my body responded to him instantly. Our kiss lingered like neither one of us wanted to break the seal, and I placed my right hand on his cheek, permitting him to give me more. He planted two more soft kisses before gently grazing my bottom lip with his teeth. I moaned, and he bit down harder. I opened my mouth as another moan escape, and he took full advantage of the opportunity. He slid his tongue inside my mouth, creating a dance to music only the two of us could hear. As if he couldn't get full access as he desired, Aeson lifted me and placed me on his lap. I was expecting to straddle him, but he cradled me instead, without breaking our kiss. I wrapped my arms around his neck as he held on to me like he was a kid holding on to his favorite teddy bear. He squeezed me tightly, with enough pressure to show how much he craved me, but not enough to hurt me. As his left arm continued to wrap around me, his right hand explored my body from massaging my scalp and teasing my locs to rubbing my back. He caressed my hips and ass, gently squeezing my thighs, traveling behind my knees. I was becoming undone while trying to etch his every move into my memory. This was a feeling I'd never experienced and never wanted to forget. I taste the mint mixed with a hint of weed on his tongue. I could smell the scent of his cologne mixing with my pheromones. Our moans and heavy breathing resounded the space as we attempted to devour each other like there was no chocolate as decadent as we were to each other.

I ran both my hands through his waves and along his neck.

Aeson gently pulled back, breaking our kiss to press his forehead against mine and whispered to me, "Talk to me, Baby. I'm feeling a lot of shit from you right now. Heavy shit. You can talk to me."

"I want you. But I don't know if we're on the same page," I admitted.

"I know what I want. And you'll get there. In the meantime, you can have me however you need, til you on what I'm on."

"You seem so sure about what you want, while all I know for now is that in order to be who someone wants, I need healing," I confessed as a tear escaped my eye.

Aeson sat me up on his lap and caressed my face while wiping my tear away. He declared, "Kalyani, I get what you're saying but you gotta heal *for you*. Worry about the rest later. But in the meantime, come here." He wrapped his arms around me so tightly, and as I hugged him back, more tears began to fall. He rubbed my back and said, "You know, there's healing in a hug too."

And with that, I made the decision to enjoy the journey. If he had me feeling like this on the first day, there had to be some good in this. If I didn't explore this thing between us, I knew I would regret it for the rest of my life. I was going to enjoy this man, even if it was just for a moment.

12

AESON

I woke up at almost five in the morning, still sitting on Ma-May's patio with Kalyani in my arms. I did not expect the night to end as it did, but I wasn't complaining. I enjoyed the smoke session with the fellas last night, but low key, I was wondering if and why Kalyani was avoiding me all of a sudden. I noticed her peeping through the kitchen blinds, and it took everything in me not laugh at her or let her know that I saw her. Just from today's encounter alone, I could tell that she was an overthinker and probably thought more of the incident with dude than it really was. Or she was embarrassed. I wasn't sure, but I also wasn't going to leave without having some clarity.

The moment I felt her in my arms, I knew this was *exactly* where she belonged. Kissing her solidified her spot and confirmed that she was the woman I was looking for. My woman. Right now, she had no idea, so I agreed to go her speed to give her time to heal and get her mind right. Past hurt made you look for the worse in a person even when they were giving their best. I was a patient man, so I didn't mind taking the time to prove myself to her. She was worth it.

I always wanted a bond like my parents. They lived by the three L's: Long lasting with lots of love and laughter. I used to think the alliteration was so corny, but as I got older, it became a mantra for me. Don't get me wrong; during high school, college, and early twenties, I played the field and slept around, but by my mid-twenties, I decided it was time to set up my life according to what I wanted my forever to look like, which was the standard they set. Unfortunately, I couldn't find anyone that I felt so strongly about that fit the standard until now.

After leaving Kalyani, I decided to go ahead and get my day started. I typically woke up around five anyway to start my workout, so there was no need to change it up. Since it was Sunday, I could take a nap later, if needed. I jumped in the shower and reminisced over the past twelve hours, more so, the last few hours. I stood under the shower head and let the hot water run over my body for a minute to adjust. I saturated my loofah with my body wash and began lathering my body, imagining Kalyani's hands caressing all over my neck, face, head, and chest. Just the thought of her had my rod at attention. The way she melted in my arms as I held her. The smoothness of her skin as I rubbed her body. The softness of her lips as I kissed her. The rising steam amplified the sensation within me. I continued to think of my sweet Kalyani. Although I managed to restrain myself with her last night, the buildup was something serious. I gripped my rod firmly and moved rhythmically, replaying her soft moans she sung in my ears. With my eyes closed, my movements became more rapid as I replayed yesterday's sequence of events and created new ones in my mind. I saw her as my woman, allowing me to please her in ways she couldn't imagine. And with that, I released down the drain.

Once my breathing reset to back to normal, I finished my shower and threw on a wifebeater, basketball shorts, and my sneakers. I scarfed down a banana and bottle of pre-workout before I headed outside for my run. The sun was just beginning to show itself, so it wasn't too hot just yet. As tired as I was, I was committed to my morning runs. I usually do five, but I would just settle for two today. That was better than nothing. With my AirPods in place, I turned on an Eric Thomas' YouTube video while I did a few quick stretches. As I stepped onto the sidewalk, I spotted Kalyani jogging across the street. It's like God was sending her to me like, "Go getcho woman!" With the quickness, I ran over to catch up with her and jogged alongside her.

Once she noticed me, she yelped, "Nigga, what the hell you doin' beside me?"

I laughed and responded, "I'm doing what I do everyday. Why you running on my block?!"

It was her turn to laugh as she said, "Nigga been here a few months and now it's your block? I run these streets, literally!"

"Well, let's get it. Two miles." I stated.

"Bet."

I adjusted the volume on my AirPods as we shifted from fast jog to run. I typically run faster when I'm alone, but we were going at a pretty good pace. As she ran, her locs bounced on top of her head. She wore a sun visor, but the sun still illuminated her beautiful brown skin. I could still see the sweat dripping down her face and neck, making her glisten, looking sexy as hell. Her breasts danced in a figure eight motion in her orange sports bra, and her toned thighs displayed their sculpture with each stride in her matching shorts. She made it hard to concentrate when I wanted to grab her and tongue her down on this same sidewalk. I picked up my pace in an effort to get slightly ahead of her, but she met me step for step. It turned into a friendly race, trying to outdo each other until we ended up back at my house.

As we tried to catch our breaths, I asked, "So what you about to get into today?"

"Nothing much. Ma-May's cooking breakfast for us this morning. I know you didn't forget."

"Nah, I didn't. I was going to text Rem to find out what time to slide through."

"Ok, good. What else do you have planned?" she questioned.

"Nothing, really. I'm supposed to chill with Remy later on, but I'm about to make a protein shake. Want one?"

She scrunched her face up at me like I said something nasty. "Girl, my shakes be bussin' bussin'! Come on and try it."

I reached out for her hand, and she accepted mine as we walked inside the house. As we scurried through the living area to get to the kitchen, I turned on an R&B playlist and "Angles" by Wale began to play softly, loud enough to be a vibe, but low enough so as to not drown out our conversation. Kalyani looked around with a look of awe on her face. I pulled out one of the island barstools for her to take a seat and began pulling out all the ingredients for our protein shakes. "What kind of fruit do you like? Any allergies?"

"No allergies. I eat pretty much all fruit except white dragon-fruit, but bananas and strawberries are my favorite."

"Ok, cool. You're gonna love this," I pulled out the bananas and strawberries from the fridge and began cutting them up.

"Your house is so beautiful. Who decorated for you?" She wanted to know.

"Thank you, but what you mean, gyal? I decorated my house." I said that shit with my chest because I was proud of my work.

She smiled and nodded in approval and started rattling off questions. "How many bedrooms are in this house? And why do you have such a big house?"

"I'll answer your fifty-leven questions but taste this first," I handed her the protein shake.

She took a sip through her straw and rolled her eyes dramatically, "Oh my Gaaawwddddd, that's so good! I'm gonna need you to make me one of these everyday!"

I licked my lips and happily said, "That can be arranged."

"You haven't answered my questions," Kalyani acknowledged, blushing.

"Ok. There's four bedrooms, four and a half bathrooms, a living room, den, man cave upstairs, and of course, a kitchen," I said with a smile.

"Oh, I just noticed the kitchen," she laughed. "But why such a big house if it's just you?"

As I finished my smoothie, I answered, "Because I believe in preparing for my future. Right now, it's just me, but my wife and kids will take over soon, and I'll be stuck in my man cave playing PlayStation 5 with my sons...or daughters."

"Wow." She spoke with wide eyes, "That's..."

"What, corny?" I posed.

"No," she said then paused. "It's admirable."

Now it was my turn to blush. "So we got some time before breakfast. Would you like a tour?"

"I was wondering if you were gonna ask," Kalyani said as she stood from the island.

"Come on, Gal."

As I took her on a quick tour of the house, we made small talk, joking about everything and anything. The tour didn't take long since I didn't have everything furnished yet. A couple of the bedrooms were still empty, and I used the den for my weights when I didn't want to workout in the garage. She fell in love with the spacious closets and bathrooms, saying how her entire townhouse could fit in the closet and still have room. We walked upstairs to the bonus room, which currently served as my game room. I had almost everything you could possibly think of wanting to play from my ping pong table to my pool table. I had a dart board on one wall and a hot shot basketball game in the corner. Along another wall was a Pac Man game arcade machine that my parents bought me for my 16th birthday. A leather couch and matching dual recliner posted up in front of the seventy-five-inch tv. The tv hung over my entertainment center that was filled with the Nintendo, Super Nintendo, Sega Genesis, and PlayStation 5, along with a bunch of games assorted accordingly.

She was like a kid in a toy store, touching everything, but I loved her excitement. Her energy was so contagious, and her laugh was sounded so goofy and sweet to my ears, that I couldn't help but imagine hearing it throughout the house on a daily basis. "Oh...my...God!! This is so dope! I am in love! Why do you have all of this?! O-M-G! Not Crash Bandicoot. Boy, what you know 'bout this?!"

As I sat in my recliner, I answered her question with a question, "If I'm gonna have a game room, I gotta have all the games I like, right?"

She glided towards me and replied, "So you like to play games, huh?" She stood directly in front of me, and though I was eye level to her belly button, I could feel her eyes burning into me. To break the magnetizing desire to grab her by the waist, I sat back in the recliner and looked up into her face. "Clouds" by Jon Vinyl began to flow from the speakers, signifying that the vibe had definitely shifted.

"Nah, baby. I only like playing games we both can win."

"Hmph, I don't know any games like that."

"Word? We just played last night." I grabbed her by the waist, pulled her onto my lap to straddle me, and kissed her soft lips. "Remember?"

"Very vaguely but feel free to refresh my memory," she teased.

I hummed the tune of "The Kissing Game" and grinned as she laughed.

"Ohhhhhh, I remember now," and she pressed her lips to mine, deepening our kiss. I pulled her hair out of her ponytail and gripped a handful of her hair, while she grabbed the sides of my head. I didn't think I'd be able to control myself like I did last night. Shit was getting real intense. The heat between her legs caused my manhood to rise at full attention, attempting to rip through the fabric of my boxers and shorts. She began grinding on top of me, and I slid my hands under her sports bra, exposing her caramel brown breasts and nipples, a shade of mahogany. They stood proudly at attention, begging for my attention, so I gently squeezed one as I licked the other. She let out a guttural moan of approval and squeezed my head between her hands. I did it again, then switched to show equal attentiveness.

I stopped to look into her eyes and hopefully see if we were going in the same direction. Her eyes were pleading with me to keep going, and I was ready to oblige. As if I was moving too slow, Kalyani took the lead and pulled the lever to recline the chair.

In her new position on top of me, she asked, "You on what I'm on?"

"Hell yeah," I replied, grabbing her by the neck to tongue her down. I, then, traveled down to her neck, kissing, sucking, and biting like I was a vampire out for blood. I didn't think we would be having sex in my recliner in the game room, but if that's what she wanted, I was with. She looked like she wanted and needed this just as much as I did, and I'd be dumb as hell to say no.

Just as she pulled my wifebeater over my head, both of our phones went off. There was a group text from Remy to us both that said, **Ma-May said bring y'all asses on for breakfast. Y'all ain't slick! And you bet not be hunchin' my sister, Nigga!**

Kalyani jumped up like he could see her through the window. "Shit! Remy makes me so sick!"

I laughed and replied to the text.

Otw.

After we redressed and got presentable, I grabbed her hand and instructed, "Let's go eat."

13

KALYANI

Aeson and I strode across the street and up the driveway, and I pouted like a kid with my head down. I wasn't ready to leave his house. I wasn't even hungry.

Aeson quizzed, "Are you ok? What's wrong?" I loved how attentive and concerned he was about my wellbeing. I could feel that he genuinely cared, and that was a major turn on for me. Hell, at this point, everything he did was a turn on. I wanted him so bad, I couldn't take it.

I replied, "No, I'm not ok. I prefer sausage over grits and eggs."

He gave me a puzzled look, so I smirked, and he burst into laughter, "Girl, you crazy as hell."

"And honest." I offered as we walked into the house.

"Well, good morning to y'all!" Ma-May spoke, bypassing me to hug and kiss Aeson. I was okay with that since I had already talked to her before leaving for my run this morning. Everyone else was still asleep at that time, but she was getting ready ready for the super early seven o'clock service. Out of all three services, she preferred that one so she could be in and out in time to cook.

Everyone was already digging into the food so I couldn't help but ask, "So y'all couldn't wait on us? I bet y'all didn't even say grace."

Eden was the first to speak with her mouth full of bacon, "Sis, I tried. I should've been on my second plate by now, so be thankful."

"You and my nephew get a pass, but not these other greedy niggas," I said while shoulder bumping Remy. PJ and DJ lifted their heads long enough to dap up Aeson and went right back to their plates.

"Girl, sit down and eat. I'm sure you called on the good Lord enough for all of us," Zena added her two cents.

Everybody thought that was so funny. Even Aeson laughed as he washed his hands at the kitchen sink. "Y'all childish." I even chuckled a bit, thinking how I probably would've been if I wasn't over here fixing grits.

When I saw him reaching for a plate, I stopped him and told him, "Have a seat. I'll fix it. What would you like?"

Aeson grinned and bit his bottom lip, then murmured in my ear, "I'll eat whatever you put on my plate."

It was my turn to bite my lip and smile, "I gotchu. I won't fix too much now, but I'll serve you your next course at your house. And that'll be buffet style."

"Word, all I can eat?" he clarified.

"And then some," I promised with lust filled eyes. Aeson kissed my forehead and went to join them in the dining area.

I noticed Ma-May sitting at the end of the table watching our exchange. It was crazy how she noticed everything. She smiled in approval, and I shook my head and laughed while fixing our plates.

After we all ate, the guys went outside for their post-breakfast blunt and the ladies cleaned up the kitchen. As I loaded the dishwasher, I turned around to find Ma-May, Zena, and Eden all staring at me with the biggest grins on their faces.

"What?!" I asked, genuinely confused.

"You guys are so cute together, Sis," Eden expressed with glossy eyes.

"Oh hell, she about to start that crying mess," Zena voiced, rolling her eyes.

"Shut up, Z. This baby makes me cry about everything."

"That man is smitten with you, Kali," Ma-May chimed in.

Before I could respond, Zena said, "You put it on him, didn't you, Cuzzi?"

"No, I did not, we just linked up on our run this morning and went back to his house for smoothies. Nothing happened."

"So what y'all been doing? Make it make sense to me, please."

"Zena, you so damn nosey." I threw the dishrag at her.

"Well, I wanna know too," asserted Eden.

"Me too," added Ma-May.

"Ma!"

"Don't '*Ma*' me. Give us the tea."

I conceded and gave them the details of last night and this morning. By the time I finished, Ma-May said, "Baby, you could've skipped this breakfast. The hell with these grits and eggs." We all laughed.

After talking for a bit, Eden decided she needed a nap on the couch and Ma-May went in her room to take a call for her Sunday afternoon gossip session. I took a quick shower, threw on a T-shirt dress, then Zena and I decided to go outside with the fellas. She wanted to smoke, but I just wanted to be near Aeson.

As soon as we stepped onto the patio, BJ passed Zena the blunt, as if they knew why she came out.

"Come sit by me," Aeson suggested, and I sat on his lap. He wrapped his arm around my waist and asked, "You good?" I nodded and smiled, and he kissed my forehead again. His level of affection was so new to me, but I loved every minute of it. He didn't care who was around, he was going to make sure I was okay.

I looked up and Remy was looking in our direction smiling and nodding his head in approval. That action spoke volumes because Remy was very protective over me, and I trusted his judgment completely. If he approved of Aeson, then this was worth exploring.

"Wanna hit the blunt with me?" Aeson asked, pulling me from my thoughts.

"No thanks. It's been so long since I've smoked, no need to start back," I responded.

"Why did you stop?" he probed.

"Because that nigga didn't want her to," Zena answered for me, minding my business. I gave her a look to tell her to shut the hell up.

She shrugged. "My bad. I was thinking it and it just blurted out. This weed must have some truth serum in it!" My cousins and brother laughed as I dropped my hand to my forehead to hide my face.

Aeson glared at me, removed my hand, and posed, "Do you wanna smoke with me?" Although he asked the same question, it seemed to have a different connotation this go round.

"Yeah, let's smoke."

We smoked and vibed with everybody for a while longer. I was high off my ass, feeling good, and wanted to feel something else. "Aes…" I hissed, looking down on him.

"Le'go," he replied, clearly understanding my words unspoken.

We stood and Aeson dapped up the guys and hugged Zena. I told them I would be back later.

Remy mentioned, "Kali, you know it's Sunday. You should bring Aeson to come vibe with us tonight."

Aeson gave me a look of confusion, and I answered his unasked question, "I'll tell you about it at the house." It took me a minute to realize why he was smiling so hard. Apparently, he liked my slip of the tongue, using "the house" instead of "your house." I ignored his silly grin as we walked back across the street.

As we approached the front door, we could hear "Read Your Mind" by Avant coming from the speakers inside. We sauntered to the kitchen and grabbed two bottles of water from the fridge. I don't know if it was from smoking or my nervousness, but my mouth was so dry that I guzzled the water down in seconds.

My phone beeped, notifying me of a text message from Remy.

> The glow looks good on you, Sis. He's a good dude. Don't base your future on your past. Live in this moment. Enjoy it. Love you Kali girl.

I smiled and simply returned.

> Love you more, Rem. [kiss emoji].

As I sat my phone on the island, Aeson moved over to me and wrapped his arms around my waist as I wrapped mine around his neck. He placed a soft kiss against my neck as he rested his head there for a moment. I never knew a hug could feel this good.

Aeson wanted to see where my head was at, asking, "Do you wanna go back upstairs to play the game?"

"Nah, we can play one in your room though. I'll make sure we both win," I flirted.

"Oh, that's what you on?" He looked so sexy with his eyes low as hell staring into mine.

I started singing Subway featuring 702's song, *"You go hide and let me seek. Let me be the one to make you weak."*

And in one swift motion, Aeson picked me up off my feet, and

I wrapped my legs around him where my arms previously took up residence. He kissed my lips, telling me, "I'm on what you on," as he carried me to his bedroom.

Once inside, I did a quick glance of the huge space. The walls were a dark gray with gray, black, and white art hanging. There was a sitting area in the corner with a black couch, coffee table, and a decorative floor lamp that also doubled as a cute bookshelf. His king size bed sat in the middle of the room with black, white, and gray bedding. I realized that we didn't come in here when he showed me around earlier, so I wondered, "So why wasn't your room a part of the tour?"

He pinned me against the wall, our bodies pressed together, and his eyes filled with lust as he gazed at me before saying, "Because we wouldn't have made it to breakfast."

I kissed him passionately, our lips meeting before he could speak. His soft, warm lips parted, and I gently explored with my tongue. He began kissing me urgently, as if I held his breath. He eventually broke the kiss and placed me on my feet and just stared as we both breathed so heavily. He kissed my forehead, then removed my locs from my signature ponytail. As he ran his fingers through, gripping my locs, I became even more undone. It had been a few months since I last had sex, so I was ready to pounce on him and take the lead, but his aura was so captivating, I had to let him do his thing. He tugged at the bottom of my dress before pulling it over my head and throwing it to the side. I stood there in my bra and panties, feeling somewhat uneasy because I had gained some pounds during my depression, but Aeson made me feel so desirable as he ran his hands up and down my body, cupping my ass and squeezing, immediately causing me to leak. He unhooked my bra, squeezed my breasts, and whispered, "You're so beautiful, Babygirl. Damn, you're so sexy."

I stood on my tiptoes to kiss his lips, offering, "Thank you, Baby," as I pulled his shirt over his head, exposing his dark, chocolate, tattoo covered chest. I kissed his chest and ran my tongue across his nipples while rubbing his abs with both my hands. My hands traveled south over the bulge in his shorts, and I felt just how well-endowed he was. My mouth watered at the idea of how big he was when hard. Before I could go any further, he lifted me up and laid me gently on the bed. He leaned back on his haunches and pulled my soaking wet panties off and threw them to the floor. Thankfully, I kept up my wax appointments.

"Ooh, she purty, Baby." He lowered his head and came back up saying, "And she smells so sweet, too. Can I taste her?" I slowly nodded my consent, as I anticipated feeling his tongue. "Wait, I wanna play with my food first. Can I play with it?" I nodded again. "Nah, we not playin' the quiet game, Kali. Let me hear that sexy ass voice. Can I play with my food first?"

"Yes, Aes. Play with it, babe."

"Bet," was all he said before sliding a finger between my folds and playing with my swollen bud. I bit my bottom lip, trying not to scream while my body damn near levitated off the bed.

He slid two fingers inside, and I immediately came. "Oh, shit, Aeson!!"

"Yeah, she almost ready for me, Baby. I gotta take my time with her. Is that okay?"

"Do whatever you gotta do, Aeson." He chuckled, hearing the frustration in my voice.

"Aye, calm that attitude down, girl. I'm gon' give you just what you want. Relax."

I attempted to roll my eyes at him until I felt his tongue breach my entrance. With his fingers still sliding in and out of me, he applied pressure as he sucked my pearl. My eyes rolled into the back of my head and my back lifted off the bed. He held each of my thighs tightly with his arms to secure me down from the waist below, while my arms searched for something to hold on to.

Aeson licked, slurped, and sucked until my dam broke, and I squirted all over him.

"Aye, that lil' thing right nih, gal," he declared while pulling out a condom from the drawer of his nightstand, stroking his erection. I held my breath with anticipation, leaning back on my elbows, hoping to catch a glimpse at what we were working with. It was hard to see with his dark complexion amidst the dark décor. A little bit of light peeked through the curtains, but it was still hard for me to see.

He climbed back into bed on top of me and kissed me gently, and expressed, "You taste so good, Kali. I gotta take my time and savor this." He kissed along my jaw line and proceeded to drag his tongue all over my neck to my collarbone. My moans managed to escape through my labored breathing. His trail continued to my shoulders then backtracked to my breasts. As he massaged one with his hand, he used his mouth to massage the other, alternating to give equal attention. The dim lighting heightened my tactile sensations, causing each touch to feel like a jolt of electricity coursing through my body. He planted wet kisses along my stomach, paying extra attention to my spot between my belly button and my mound. I was unraveling audibly as another orgasm pierced through my body. He lapped up every drop of my juices with his tongue before sliding his thick erection up and down my slit, as if to familiarize himself with the area. If he was already feeling this good just rubbing against me, I anxiously and excitedly feared how amazing he was going to feel once he slid inside, like a kid waiting on a roller coaster ride.

Unable to take any more of the teasing, I damn near begged, "Please, Aeson. Please put it in."

He let out a guttural groan as he thrust inside of me. "Gotdamn, Kali! This shit feels so good, Babygirl."

I damn near clawed my nails into his back as he stroked me senseless. The sound of our moans, kissing, and thighs slapping against each other drowned out the music coming from the speakers. He threw my legs over his shoulders and continued to pound me into another orgasm.

Once I came down, I pressed against his chest and uttered, "Let me ride." We switched positions without him even pulling out, but once I was on top, I wanted to feel him reenter. With my feet planted firmly on the bed and my hand against his chest, I rose and lowered myself on his shaft, feeling every one of the many inches expanding my walls. I rode Aeson until we both climaxed, and I fell against his chest, dozing in and out of consciousness.

14

AESON

As we laid in my bed, I wrapped my arms around her and kissed her shoulder. I was already feeling her so much, and the sex just made me want her even more. I know I said I'd meet her where she was at, but I could already see that it was going to be a struggle trying not to fall in love with her. She had such a beautiful spirit that made me want to be connected to her, and the sex was so bomb, I didn't want her to go home. Shit, she could move in tonight.

Interrupting my thoughts, she announced, "Aes, I'm not a ho, okay?"

"Ummm, okay. Who said you were one?" I asked for clarification.

"Nobody, but I'm just saying. I'm not the type to sleep with someone that I just met yesterday. Like, seriously, we don't even know much about each other yet, but it feels so weird with you. Like I know you but don't know you at the same time. And you make me feel so comfortable and desired. I just want to get out of my head and enjoy you."

"Are you enjoying yourself so far?"

"Hell, yeah! You already know!" She giggled.

"Good." I replied. "Let's play a game."

"You really like games, don't you?" Kalyani mused.

"I like to have fun. And since you say you don't know me, ask me three questions about myself. But the kicker is, you have to answer those same questions about yourself. That way you won't feel like a *ho* next time."

She gasped and turned around so quickly to face me and smacked my chest, "Nigga!"

"What?! Those were your words, not mine!"

"You better be glad I like the idea. My first question is...how old are you?"

"I'll be thirty-five on August 5th," I answered.

"Okay, Leo. Mine is October 13th. I'll be thirty-one. How many siblings do you have?"

"My big brother Reece lives in Sacramento. No other siblings."

"We're similar there, except Remy lives ten minutes away from me. What made you move here?"

I paused a moment before answering. "Well, I have to give you a little backstory to answer that question. I grew up very family oriented. My parents had the best relationship, ya know? I always saw them dancing, playing, adoring each other, and having fun, so I always wanted what they had."

"Had?" Kalyani was confused and curious.

"Yeah, my dad passed away six years ago, and my mom managed to make it another four years before she died of a broken heart," I recounted.

With tear-filled eyes, Kalyani rubbed my arm as she apologized for my loss.

"It's cool. These things happen. At least I got to experience them for as long as I did. They taught me a lot, but just by watching them, I learned what love really is. Now, to answer your question, I moved because I was living in their memory rather than living in honor of them. I needed a change of scenery so that their absences wouldn't hurt so much, and the job opportunity was too sweet to pass up."

"So you moved to Mayberry?"

"I ain't lyin'! But for real though, I love it out here. This neighborhood is for a family, and like I told you earlier, I'm preparing for that."

"What if your wife doesn't want to live here?" she challenged.

"She will, but if she ever decides that she wants to move, that's a discussion that we will have and compromise on." Kali seemed impressed by my response. "Now, you've asked your three questions, so it's my turn. What happened in your last relationship?"

"Ughhhh," she rolled her eyes and continued. "Long story short, I met him at my job, gave him a chance when I knew better. Things were cool for a little minute then he became mentally and verbally abusive. Oh, apparently, he was cheating on me majority of the relationship."

"Ok, that explains some things from yesterday. So how long were y'all together?"

"Five years. I broke it off a couple months ago. Yesterday was the first time I saw him since we split." She sat up, pressing her back against the headboard and crossing her arms, visibly uncomfortable. I sat up beside her, not touching, but close enough for her to know I was there for her. She leaned her head on my shoulder, saying, "That relationship drained me, broke me, and made me lose sight of who I was. No matter how hard I tried, I couldn't do anything right, and I just wasn't enough for him. And I took it and tried to do better because maybe he was right. Then I just grew numb to the bullshit. Like, bruh. I had nothing left in me. Once he raised his hand to hit me, I was completely done.

And now I'm left trying to rebuild me. It's just going to take time."

"I hate you had to experience that, but I wish I would've known he tried to put his hands on you. I would've boxed his ass last night."

"He wouldn't have been worth it, but I thank you anyway. So what about your last relationship?"

"Real shit, I haven't been in a legit relationship in about seven years. It lasted a couple years, but ended because she wasn't ready to settle down like I was. I couldn't blame her though. At least she was honest instead of wasting my time. Since then, I've talked to women, dated, had casual sex, but nothing serious. I've really just been focused on moving and adjusting to a new environment."

"Oh really? So you haven't talked to any women since you've moved here?" Kalyani had her arms crossed and gave me a look daring me to lie.

"I didn't say that. I've met a couple women, but nothing serious...or sexual. Just a little chatting here and there. A date or two."

"Why nothing more?"

Staring into her eyes, I answered, "Because when you know, you know. And when it ain't, you let 'em go."

"I like that," she smiled.

"So, my final question," I placed my arm around her shoulders. "Tell me what you wanted to be when you grew up versus what you became."

"Mmmmm, that's a good one." She paused and thought about it for a second. "As a little kid, I dreamed of being a singer like Whitney Houston when I was little, but I can't sing worth a damn. Then I changed it to a songwriter and spoken word artist, like the ones that do poetry slams. I ended up becoming a bank manager."

"What happened to the dream?" I wanted to know.

"The songwriting wasn't really my thing, and spoken word was more like a hobby while in college. I still do it sometimes though. It's a coincidence that we're on this topic though. Remember when Remy said you should hang with us? He's referring to poetry night in Layton."

"Oh, word? I don't believe in coincidences, but timing is everything. If you're inviting me, I'd love to go."

"Cool, we can ride together then."

"Am I gonna see you on your *Love Jones* shit tonight?"

"I doubt it, but it'll be a vibe. I promise."

"Let's find me something to wear then."

I pulled Kali from the bed and grabbed her a t-shirt to throw on and me some boxers. We went inside my walk-in closet, where she picked out a mauve button up shirt, light denim jeans, and white Forces. I paired them with a simple gold chain, watch, and diamond earrings.

Since her clothes were at her house in Layton, we agreed to leave early and get dressed there.

I kissed her neck, coaxing, "Let's get it in one more time before we head out."

15

KALYANI

"You know you owe me an answer, right?" I reminded Aeson as he drove to my townhouse.

"What you mean?" he pondered.

"What did you want to be when you grew up versus software development?"

"I wanted to be a gym teacher," he said without taking his eyes off the road.

"Oh, really?!"

"Yeah, I love kids. And gym was the best class in school. Always lit!"

"You right, you right. So why the change the heart?" I continued my line of questioning.

"I followed the money. I figured I would get the best of both worlds coaching little league for my kids, but that hasn't happened yet. There's still time though."

"That is so damn sweet, Aes," I endorsed, grinning ear to ear. "Maybe Zena can help you with that. She's a middle school teacher and coaches city league sometimes."

"Zena?!" He gazed at me in shock, and I laughed.

"Don't do my cousin. She's a nut, but she loves the kids, nih."

"That's what up. I'll definitely holla at her about that."

We stopped for smoothies and sandwiches before arriving at my house. We only had a few hours until Remy and Zena arrived since we decided that we could all ride together. Eden decided that she was too pregnant for late night shenanigans, so she wasn't going to make it.

Once we entered, Aeson complimented my décor and asked, "So are you going to give me a tour?"

"There's two bedrooms and two baths. My place could fit inside of yours."

"So what? It's yours. And you clearly love it. So I want to see."

I took him on a quick tour before returning to the living room and grabbing two dinner trays so that we could eat on the couch. As we ate, we got more acquainted with each other. We were vibing so hard, I almost wanted to say forget our plans, let's just stay here, but he seemed pretty excited about it.

I let Aeson pick out my outfit for the night since I picked out his, and he did not disappoint with the denim jeans, flowy, white blouse, and open toe heels. Then, we laid across the bed for a quick nap because we were both exhausted. Spending the day with him had been amazing, and lying in his arms was so peaceful. As I drifted off to sleep, I wondered what life would be like with him as my man. What if I was good enough to be his woman? And with that thought, I drifted off.

An hour later, I awoke to Aeson playing "When I See You" by Fantasia on my TV. Loudly. As hell.

Opening my eyes, I saw Aeson holding the remote control as if he was performing on stage.

"OMG…you are so damn silly!"

"I tried to wake you, but you were sleeping so hard. I

would've thought you were in a coma if it wasn't for the snoring."

"I do not snore!" I yelled, throwing a pillow at him.

"Okay, my little freight train. Ready to jump in the shower?" He grabbed my hands for me to stand, pulled me into a hug, and kissed my forehead.

"Yeah, you're taking it with me, right?" I hoped I didn't seem desperate, but I wasn't ready to separate from him even for that short amount of time.

"Shit, yeah." He confirmed before kissing my lips.

The second we stepped into the walk-in shower, Aeson began kissing the back of my neck and shoulders. He grabbed my loofah and body wash and began washing my body. I tried to watch him and take it all in, but I had to close my eyes as he moved so tenderly and deliberate. He washed my body like I was fragile. Not broken egg fragile, but fine china or crystals. He was taking care of me, and that thought alone made my eyes swell.

Once I was rinsed off, I returned the favor, trying to emulate his actions, but his sexiness was a distraction. The pheromones wafted in the air mixed in the steam, and I wanted him to experience the same pleasure he was giving me. I lowered to wash his long legs and saw his member rising, up close and personal.

Even as the water cascaded along his body, I could still see its beauty. This man was literally a work of art from head to toe, but extra time and creativity was put into creating that rod. The long, thick, veiny, chocolate decadence was so mouthwatering that I couldn't resist running my tongue against the veins. I began to lick all over, practically French kissing his erection. Before I could really go in, I heard banging on the bathroom door.

BANG. BANG. BANG.

"What the hell y'all doing?! Y'all had all day to hunch! Let's go!" Zena called out.

"Zena, please!! We're coming! Damn!" I hailed back.

Aeson kissed my lips, refocusing my thoughts, "Come on, baby. To be continued later."

About forty-five minutes later, we were dressed and on our way to Esmee's Coffee & Vibes. On the way, we filled Aeson in on who she was and what to expect. Esmee was Zena's cousin on her dad's side and practically grew up with us so we called her cousin also. A few years ago, she opened a storefront coffee bar in downtown Layton. Esmee's wasn't like your average Starbucks but more like Central Perk on the show *Friends*.

The shop had reading nooks, couches, work areas, served breakfast and lunch, and even rented out space in the back for exercise classes, yoga, and more. I actually taught Zumba a couple evenings a week, and last year, she decided she wanted to add live entertainment on Sunday nights, and it had been very successful so far.

We could see quite a few people piling in as we parked but weren't too concerned since it was relatively early. The word was spreading so more and more people were coming out on Sundays, causing limited seating because Esmee always reserved us a section.

Once parked, Aeson came around to open my door and held my hand for me to get out, giving me a look like he could attack at any time, and I would've definitely let him.

"Thank you, Aeson."

"You're so welcome, Kalyani."

We looked up to see Remy and Zena cheesing like two proud parents watching their kids go to prom.

"Y'all look fine as hell together! Damn!" Zena complimented.

"I can't front. Y'all really do look good together," Remy agreed.

We both blushed, very embarrassed by this whole interaction.

"Say 'Cheese,'" Zena directed before snapping our picture.

16

AESON

As we journeyed through the parking lot, I intentionally walked a couple steps behind Kali just to admire her. She looked absolutely gorgeous. The outfit I picked out was sexy as hell on her. She wasn't too revealing, but there was enough skin showing from her shoulder to her thighs to make my mouth water.

The orange polish on her nails and toes complemented her skin and the brown heels adorning her feet. She embellished the fit with gold accessories, like me. Her locs were loosely hanging like I liked and swung freely with every stride. Her makeup was light, but her lips were glossed with a little bit of that ombre liner stuff, making her full lip look even more plump. I was too honored to be on her arm tonight.

As we entered, they all hugged and greeted a woman with a familiar face, standing by the door. As I as trying to place her, Kalyani introduced us.

"Esmee, this is my friend, Aeson. Aeson, this is our cousin Esmee, the owner that I was telling you about."

"Hi, Aeson. I remember you from the party. Good to meet you, and welcome to Esmee's Coffee & Vibes."

"Pleasure to meet you," I conveyed while shaking her hand. "You have a dope spot here."

"Thank you so much. You all can have a seat in your usual area, and a waitress will be with your shortly."

We headed to a booth with big plush leather seats that had a great view of the stage area. Within minutes, a waitress appeared with menus, ready to take our drink order.

"Hey, y'all! Welcome to Esmee's. What can I get you all to drink?"

"Water for now," Zena said.

"Same," Kali replied.

"I'll take a house punch," Remy ordered.

"I'll just take a pineapple juice," I placed my drink order. As I looked up towards the waitress, I recognized her immediately as a woman I had gone on a date with soon after moving to town. "Hey, Veronica. How you doing?" I asked casually.

"Well, hi, Aeson. Long time no see," she replied as she looked back and forth between Kalyani and me. "Well, I'll be right back with your drinks," she stated before taking off to the bar.

Everyone looked at me as if waiting for a response. "I met her at the gym when I first moved to town. Nothing major."

That explanation seemed to work for Rem and Zena, but Kali observed me a little longer as if to see if there was a glimpse of a lie in my eyes. I reassured her by saying, "When you know, you know," placing a kiss on her forehead, and she visibly relaxed. Veronica and I grabbed lunch once but the vibe wasn't really there. The conversation was forced and we didn't have much in common besides the gym. Before letting something fester that was leading nowhere, I let her know how I felt and ended it before it started.

She must've felt some type of way because a different waitress was bringing our drinks. We placed our orders just as Esmee took the stage to introduce herself and welcome everyone.

In between the artists she introduced, a live band played instrumentals. Some artists in the audience did covers to songs, giving us a karaoke vibe. This was different from anything I'd ever been attended, and I was loving it. After three months, I realized this was what I was missing: a social life and friends to hang out with. Although I'd known Remy since I started working and we'd gone out with our coworkers, this was different. More personal. More genuine.

To say Kali wasn't ready for a relationship, her actions showed differently. She was very affectionate and playful, even eating some of my wings off my plate. And babygirl sucked the bone clean, down to the gristle. Having that level of comfortability spoke volumes to me even if her mouth didn't utter the words.

Esmee returned to the stage to announce the next artist. "Everyone, our next artist isn't new here, but she's not quite a regular. She started using this platform to release her frustrations but ended up unleashing her gifts upon us all. Please welcome Kalyani to the stage!"

I slid out of the booth and helped her up on the platform. As she took the mic, I stood front and center. I gave her a look, asking if it was okay, and as if she totally understand me, she gave a quick nod and smirk. She didn't tell me she was performing, but I was hoping that she would, and I didn't want to miss a word.

"Scared to move. Like I'm weak. Like I'm paralyzed. Paralyzed with fear.
This must be the feeling when you take your first step after being
immobile for so long.
Fear of falling.
Maybe I'm not supposed to move just yet. I haven't healed completely.

Fear of moving too fast. Wrong timing.
But what's gonna happen when I leave all this behind?
Fear of the past.
What's gonna come at me when I go?
Will there be anybody waiting for me?
Anybody to help me?
What if I never heal?
Fear of the future. I can't win for losing!
The gallons of fear has kept me stagnant while the ounce of hope
attempts to swim at the surface.
Gasping for air, begging not to drown. I literally feel the gasping. The
choking.
I'm treated like I don't know what I want when that's so untrue.
I know what I want, but fear that my wants don't want me back.
That I'm chasing a desire that's running from me.
That I can never just walk in peace but always running towards the
unreachable.
So I stay.
Complacent.
Unhappy.
Confused.
And I'm SCARED.
Not of my own capabilities because I know there's a power I possess.
But that my power won't be enough.
It hasn't been this far.
What makes this time different?
Just scared."

Seeing her in her element was amazing. Her expressions, her mannerisms, the passion, the words she spoke...this was her element and I was so proud to be able to share this moment with her. After helping Kalyani down, I hugged her and urged her to, "Just do it scared, Baby."

We continued to enjoy the show until it was close to midnight. Afterwards, we all headed back to Kali's where we split ways. I wasn't sure if she wanted to stay at her place or head back to Bay Springs, but her truck was still at Ma-May's. As soon as we walked inside we both fell on the couch.

"Thank you for inviting me tonight. It was dope and you were fire up there. I enjoyed everything."

"Thank you for accepting the invitation. Really, thank you for a great weekend. I haven't felt this good in awhile."

"My pleasure, Baby. If you don't mind me asking, when did you write that poem?"

"Before my run yesterday," she answered before changing the subject. "Do you wanna call off work with me tomorrow? I'm not ready to come up from this just yet."

"I feel the same. I have a couple things that I have to do first thing in the morning, but I can do them from home."

"Ok good. Let's go back to your place then."

As soon as we got to my house, we took another shower together, but this one was different from earlier. For once, I had no music blasting. The soft sound of the water falling combined with the rising steam created a calmness and tranquility amidst our thoughts and feelings. As she leaned back into my embrace, I felt the warmth of her skin, as I wrapped my arms around her waist. I kissed her temple to ease the emotions running rampant in her mind and mine. I had never felt this way before or experienced such a high level of intimacy, but I wanted to explore the depths of this connection and vulnerability with someone who soothed my soul like Kalyani.

After showering, I threw on some boxers and gave her a t-shirt and boxers to sleep in. We drifted off to sleep as soon we settled into bed.

17

KALYANI

I woke up to 6lack "B4L" blasting through the speakers. I loved music, but first thing in the morning? Thankfully, we had similar tastes, so I could get used to it. Just the thought of being open to the idea of getting used to music at 7am spoke volumes. I went to the bathroom, took care of my hygiene then went on a hunt in the house to find Aeson. Passing by the kitchen, I noticed some takeout boxes on the counter. It smelled so good, but I wanted him more than the food.

I found him in his office sitting at his desk, shirtless with plaid pajama pants, appearing to be hard at work.

"Good morning," I whispered, not wanting to interrupt him.

He turned to me and smiled. He wore glasses?! Aeson was so damn fine. The Lord Almighty did a perfect work with this man for sure.

"I never knew I had a glasses kink until now," I let slip, biting my lip.

He mimicked my action and motioned for me to come closer. Once I stood in front of him, he pulled me on to his lap and kissed my lips.

"Word? Guess I'll have to wear them more often. I have some fetishes of my own we can explore," he countered while pulling the t-shirt over my head.

To hell with that breakfast.

LATER THAT AFTERNOON, I finally headed back to Layton. I hated to leave Aeson, but I had an appointment with my therapist. Plus, I didn't want him to get sick of me too soon. I had been seeing Monika biweekly for almost a year, and she offered a lot of insight and support regarding my relationships and mental health. I called her my "Rent-a-Bestie." She was a beautiful, dark-skinned woman about ten years older than me. She wore her sandy brown hair in a huge fro with big hoop earrings and always dressed down in her professional attire.

Her office space was so bright and welcoming with colorful hues of yellow, orange, pink, and mint greens. Soft R&B instrumental music played throughout, enhancing the relaxed energy.

"Hi, Ms. Gibson. Monika is ready for you now."

"Thank you, Chloe."

I walked into the office and greeted Monika with our usual greeting of a hug and casual conversation.

"What's new with you?"

"Soooooooo, there's this guy..."

I gave her the rundown of how Aeson and I met in the grocery store to him being Remy's coworker, Lucas showing up to the party, running together, poetry night, the connection, the vibe, the sex, everything.

After I took a break for air, Monika jumped right in, "So how does he make you feel?"

"I feel all the things when I see him."

"All the things?" she asked, needing more details.

"ALL. THE. THINGS."

"So, what's the problem?"

"What if this isn't real? What if it's emophilia or Nightingale Syndrome? What if I'm just in limerence and don't really like him?" Just the thought of Aeson and I not being real brought tears to my eyes.

"Kalyani, I won't lie to you. It could be any of those things. I don't believe it is, but I can't say for certain. And neither can you. These are things you find out over time. But you don't stop living your life and enjoying experiences based on the what ifs or worst-case scenarios you've conjured up in your head."

"Answer this for me. Why was it so easy for you to accept the mistreatment from Lucas but second guess the adoration from Aeson?"

"I didn't do anything to deserve it." And just like that, the waterworks began.

"No, you didn't deserve the mistreatment and abuse. You deserve to be adored and respected. Always. Let that man love you."

"Monika, I'm so broken, I gotta heal before I can even think about a relationship with him."

"Kalyani, honey. I hate to be the one to tell you, but you're already in a relationship with him. Your head and heart just aren't on the same level of understanding it because you've put up a wall to protect yourself from yourself and anybody else. You have made so much progress, and I love this for you, but you can't always do it alone."

"The same way medicine can help heal, so can love. He can help heal places you didn't even realize were still broken. Just give him a chance and enjoy the experience, okay?"

I nodded in agreement.

"Now remember, depression can have an onset at any time. Make sure you're staying active, repeating your affirmations, and speaking life into yourself. Keep taking your supplements, although I'm sure you're getting plenty Vitamin D!"

18

AESON

Over the next three weeks, Kali and I had gotten very close, and she was starting to let her guard down with me. Every free moment we had was spent together, whether working out, game nights, dinner dates, or just relaxing at her place or mine. Ma-May made it her mission to feed me almost everyday, whether Kali was around or not, which I truly appreciated. I really missed my mom, so her mothering nature was comforting. I'd spoken to her parents a little, but they really didn't seem to be interested, and I wasn't one to force things. Kali explained how strained their relationship was and how they really thought her ex was good for her. She never told them the extent of the abuse she endured, so they only saw it from the outside looking in. I guess I couldn't fault them for that.

Remy and I had become closer as well, considering we saw each other a lot now. I loved how he didn't pry into our relationship but encouraged it. That actually surprised me considering how close they were, but he told me that there were boundaries that he couldn't cross. As long as his sister was happy, he'd never overstep, but we could always call him when we needed his two cents.

As far as the relationship, nothing was really defined. We just *were*. She was something like my woman but quickly becoming my best friend. I wasn't big on having gray areas, but I knew Kali needed time, and I'd rather wait while still experiencing her than disconnect to let her figure it out.

Kali texted me on my lunch break:

> Kali: Hey, Mr. Wallace! How's your day going?

> Me: Hey, Ms. Gibson. I'm chillin'. Missing you tho

> Kali: I'm glad to hear it!

> Me: How's yours going?

> Kali: Busy, but productive

> Kali: May I take you out on a date tonight?

> Me: You damn sure can

> Kali: Good. I'll pick you up around 6:30pm. Wear something sexy!

> Me: Lmao! You do the same

Kali ended the conversation with a kissing emoji. That shit was so sexy to me. Don't get me wrong, I didn't mind catering to her and would always do so, but her initiating a date showed a level of care for me that I appreciated. She was strategic with it, too. Since Fridays were my half days at work, I went to the barbershop right after, so she knew I would be fresh as hell for our date tonight.

~

REMY and I walked into the barbershop, dapping up and greeting everybody. My barber, Slim, was just finishing up a client and giving him change, so I sat in his chair and waited for them to finish up their transaction. Slim was an older gentleman in his fifties and kept me lined up perfectly, just like I like. He always talked like an old school uncle, dropping knowledge.

"What's the move tonight, Aes?"

"I gotta date tonight, so you gotta get me right," I told him.

"You know that ain't no thang. Where are you taking her?"

"I really don't know. She's taking me," I answered proudly. The guys in the shop seemed to be shocked by my answer.

"Word?!" stated another barber.

"Well, damn," said his client.

"That's wassup!" I don't even know who said that.

Remy interjected, "That's my sister. What y'all niggas thought?!" We all erupted in laughter.

Slim continued to say, "Don't get me wrong, it's important for us, as men, to show up for our ladies, but when that woman steps up to take the lead so you can relax and enjoy the ride, it does something to a man. Our chest sticks out further."

"It's all about reciprocity though. You clearly make her feel loved and desired enough to want to reciprocate the action. How she treats you is a testament for how she's being treated."

The guys agreed, and you could see some of them in deep thought reflecting on what he said.

"I gotta make your line up extra crispy now!"

AS I PICKED out my outfit for the evening, I felt like a kid going on his first date. I chose a mint green, fitted two-piece suit with a white shirt and loafers. I accented with a gold belt, bracelet, watch, and necklace. I kept my diamond studs in and even threw on my dad's gold ring that I didn't wear often. I know she loved my glasses, so I wore my gold trimmed frames. I was a sexy, chocolatey ass nigga and couldn't wait to see how Kali matched my fly.

DING. DING. DING.

I heard my doorbell ring and checked my phone. Kali stood at my door with a small gift bag in her hand, smiling hard into the camera. Barely able to contain my excitement, I opened the door and picked her up in one swift motion. I placed one long kiss on her lips, trying not to smudge her lipstick.

"Damn, Baby. You look amazing!" she praised while examining me from head to toe.

"And so do you. That thing lookin' right, babe," I scanned her over with lust filled eyes.

She had on a coral halter dress that puffed out around her mid-thigh and some stilettos. Her hair and makeup were freshly done, and her lips were a sexy nude ombre. I almost wanted to forego this date and take her straight to the bedroom.

"I got you a gift," she handed me the bag.

I opened it and fell out laughing. "Kali, you really brought me a 3.5 and some cigars?"

"Yeah, I figured that's the only flower you would want. Now let's go because our reservation is at seven."

Kali took me to a rooftop restaurant in downtown Layton that I had heard about and actually intended on taking her, and everything was delicious. The ambiance was right for a sensual romantic evening.

While waiting on our entrees, Kali grabbed my hand, checking in, "Are you enjoying our date?"

"I really am. Thank you so much for everything. This was very thoughtful of you," I answered, giving her hand a little squeeze.

"Well, since we met, you've done nothing but taken care of

and looked out for me. You've been patient and so endearing. You deserve this and so much more. I've been waiting for the other shoe to drop, but you've stayed ten toes down, so consistent and genuine. And purposed."

"Purposed, huh?" I repeated, thinking about her word choice.

"Yes, you had a purpose in my life. You helped me heal with a hug. And I love you for that. And I hope you know you're my boyfriend now."

"I love you too, Kalyani," I admitted before kissing her lips.

"You were already my baby. I just needed you to catch up."

She closed her eyes and leaned her head forward, triggering me to plant a kiss on her forehead.

Neither one of us were big drinkers so we drank wine, but you would've thought we were drunk the way we danced and enjoyed each other. We were a whole vibe together, and now we were *officially* together.

Once we made it back to my house, Kali called herself walking me to my door.

"This is the end of the date. I'm supposed to make sure you make it in safely." This girl was so goofy and adorable.

Playing along, I went for it. "Would you like to come in for a nightcap?"

"Sure, I can stay for a minute," she assured before passing me and sliding inside.

As soon as I closed the door, I pushed her against it and kissed her fervently, igniting a spark that sent chills down her body and illuminating our souls. Pouring all of my unspoken desires and love into our embrace, I tried to convey my emotions in a language only our hearts could understand.

Her actions and words today showed that she trusted me to be the man that I said I was, and that meant more than I could express. I was confident in who I was and what I wanted but knowing what I wanted and hitting thirty-five, I started to question things a time or two. Now that we were official, it was time for me to step my game up and continuously show her why she made the right decision.

I unzipped the back of her dress and let it fall to the floor. I stepped back to admire her beautiful body, then hoisted her up, with her heels still in place. Taking her into my bedroom, I laid her on the bed before I quickly undressed and proceeded to make love to my woman.

19

KALYANI

O f all the days, my assistant branch manager became sick when I had little to no sleep. Aeson and I were up half the night celebrating our new relationship status and planned to chill out all day, aside from having lunch with Ma-May. But here I was at work. Thankfully, we closed at two o'clock on Saturdays, but I still didn't want to be there.

Closing the door to my office I laid my head on the desk until I heard a knock at the door.

"Kalyani, we have a client who wants to discuss a business account with you."

"Ok, Simone. You can send them in," I told her as I gathered myself.

"She can see you now," I heard her say, before Lucas walked into my office.

Every part of my being wanted to curse his ass out from A to Z, but I was the branch manager and needed to conduct myself as such.

"What do you want?" I asked, attempting to appear unbothered.

"Kali, I just want to apologize. I am so sorry for the way I treated you. You didn't deserve any of it. I know that now."

"Ok, apology heard. You may leave."

"Baby, please. I need you, Kali. I took you for granted, and I'm sorry. I disrespected you because I didn't know how to love you. I know better now."

"Lucas, listen to me, and listen to me closely. I appreciate the apology if it's sincere, but it's not my job to give you another chance to try and get it right after you royally fucked up. You made me feel like I wasn't enough, and I was asking for too much, when it was simple. And it took another man showing me that I deserved more than just the basics."

He looked at me with remorseful eyes and asked, "So you want to throw all those years away? We can make this work."

"I can't give you another chance, but I can give you advice for your next relationship. Be honest. Be fair. Give her a chance to make decisions, grow, and learn. Give her a chance to be a woman. Now leave my office, and don't come back."

Without another word, he left. And I grabbed my purse and went home to my man.

"I'm glad you're all in love and stuff, but I miss my damn cuzzy," Zena noted as she hugged me.

"Even though we talk everyday, I miss you too," I replied hugging her just as tightly.

"It hits different, but regardless, I am so happy for you and Aeson. Look how far you've come. That man went from your supermarket superhero to the lover of your soul, honey. You know I love it if you got me cooking and shit for him."

We were going on a mini baecation on his birthday weekend for the two of us to celebrate, so my family and I decided to throw Aeson a pre-birthday kickback in the rec room. It was actually Ma-May's idea. They grew remarkably close over the past month, and I loved the bond that they had. It gave us all peace of mind to know that they had someone looking out for them right across the street.

He even formed a great relationship with my parents, causing our relationship to get better. Aeson, Remy, and my dad would have their card nights while us ladies cooked dinner. He was growing on everyone, and I loved how they loved him.

My family pitched in to contribute to the party with food and decorations, and it looked so beautiful. Aeson had informed me that he didn't like surprises, so I didn't even bother to try it. He was fully aware of the plans and shut me down every time I tried to be over the top. He just wanted to vibe with the family, and that's just what he got.

As my aunts brought out the cake, I got everyone's attention, yelling, "Everybody, please gather around and sing 'happy birthday' to my bae."

We all gathered around Aeson and sang. Once he blew out the candles, I asked, "Did you make a wish?"

Before he could answer, an unfamiliar voice responded, "You must've wished for me to appear!"

20

AESON

I couldn't believe my ears or my eyes. My brother, Reece, was actually here. It was like looking in a mirror.

"What are you doing here, man?" We embraced so tight, as tears rolled down my eyes. This was so overwhelming.

"Sis reached out and made it happen," Reece replied as he gave Kalyani a side hug.

I blinked back tears as she winked at me. "Yeah, had me stealing your phone, sneaking in FaceTimes in the middle of the night! Thank God we have trust," causing everyone to laugh.

I pulled Kalyani in for a hug and kissed her lips, "Thank you so much, Baby. For everything."

"You're welcome, Baby. You deserve it and then some."

As the party continued, we played games, ate food, and just enjoyed each other. Everyone fell in love with Reece, especially Ma-May, and I know he felt the overwhelming sense of family just like I did.

Before everyone started to pack up, I called everyone's attention. "I just want to thank you all for embracing me into your family and treating me like your own. For everything I thought I was missing, you all have given it to me one hundred times over. Thank you for celebrating with me today and for every contribution. I appreciate it all."

"Kalyani, baby, I thank you so much for shopping at your local Publix." Everyone erupted into laughter.

"Seriously, I didn't know how God was going to do it, but I trusted Him to align my life as my heart desired, and he sent me you. I thank you for giving us a chance to explore our purpose and for you finally accepting the fact that I'm *that* dude. I just need you to accept one more thing." I pulled a ring box out of my pocket and dropped to my knee. "Will you accept my proposal to be my wife?"

With tears streaming down her face, Kalyani heartily replied, "I'm on what you on."

I slid her ring on her finger, and before kissing her deeply, I retorted, "When you know, you know."

EPILOGUE
AESON (ONE YEAR LATER)

Kalyani and I walked into Esmee's and headed to Remy, Eden, and Zena at our usual spot. Over the past year, Esmee's had quickly become my favorite hangout spot. I looked forward to Family Sundays which consisted of church, dinner, and poetry night. Remy and I would even come during the week to hang with the guys after work.

After a few months of begging, Kali finally persuaded me to sing, and I enjoyed it. Especially when I would sing vocals behind her poetry. Music and poetry became one of our unified love languages, always writing, reciting, and singing to one another. Working out was the other.

With all the wedding planning, we needed every opportunity that we could get to enjoy ourselves. Although it didn't matter to me, Kali wanted everything to be perfect. Since I didn't have much family, we opted for a destination wedding and a reception to follow. Kalyani was working tirelessly to get all the details squared away. I did what I could to help, but her girls help her the most With only a couple months until the big day, we both needed this break.

"Whatchu singing tonight, Aes?" Esmee asked as she hugged us both.

"I'm just twiddle-dee'ing behind Kali tonight." I replied.

"I know that's gonna be dope. The people love it when y'all perform together. Y'all are our local celebs around here."

"Yep, like BeBe and CeCe of poetry!" Zena blurted.

"Girl! If you don't shet up!" Kalyani laughed

"It really is sultry and seductive, y'all," Eden added, while sipping her tea. I tried to get Remy to sing a little bit, but he might have to do the poetry part. My baby sounds like a billy goat trying to hit them notes. Made my baby cry and all."

Remy rose from the couch as we laughed at his expense. "Y'all just a bunch of haters. The baby is too! Act like Aeson the only man that can sing. Tuh! I'm going to the bathroom."

We laughed even harder as he walked away.

A few months back, Esmee decided to let her staff takeover more of the Poetry Night duties so that she could actually enjoy herself, so she hung with us most of the time and performed occasionally.

As the night progressed, a few friends, coworkers, and regulars came over to vibe with us, filling our section to capacity. A few artists already performed, and it was winding down to our time to join the stage.

Just then, the emcee announced, "Next up, we will have our own D'Angelo and Rhapsody come to the stage, "Aesonnnnnnnn on the vocals and Kalyaniiiiiii with the verses."

A New Energy

As I inhale the air that turns to breath, I feel a shift in motion.
With every inhale, I take in newness and wholeness.
With every exhale, I let go of hurt and fear.
With every inspire, I'm inspired. I'm encouraged. I'm moved.
With every respire, I'm relaxed. I'm strengthened. I'm matured.

I embody peace like no other with a discernment that quickly alerts me when disruption is approaching.
I embody agility as I move from start to finish, switching hats like fitted to a fedora, stepping high whether in my all-white forces or in my stilettos, yet always covered and keeping pace.
I embody fortitude as I stand firm on my beliefs and focused on my desires.
Flexing but never bending to concede to another.
I embody an energy that is felt as I approach and still lingers when I leave.
An energy that sways with my hips and leads in the stride.
An energy unmatched yet interlocking with the kindred like a fresh retwist.
A new year, same me tho. Multiply by three tho.
Tap into this untapped energy...

We played around onstage per usual, just vibing with the band and freestyling, passing the mic to different people in the crowd. The mic ended up in Esmee's hand, and the beat changed. She came up on stage with us, and with a smile on her face, began to recite:

If I could rearrange the letters in the alphabet, I would put "U" and "I" together.
Corny, right?
In reality, not speaking figuratively. If I can have you, I'd have you for eternity.
This mental stimulating, emotionally captivating,
soul stirring, heart flustering, sexually invigorating vibe-
Baby, this is more than a vibe.
This is fated. Kismet. Like pure renaissance.
You took the shattered pieces, and with your words, revived this art.
With your touch, you rewrote literature.

From a self-help book to infamous publication.
I give you your creds because you undoubtedly revised pages of hurt,
fear, anguish, resentment, desertion
And manifested, unsurfaced, tapped into an essence untouched.
A story untold.
A love level only imagined, once imitated, never mastering the
underlying qualities
But laying atop the surface as a cover, masking the brilliance that lies
underneath.
You unearthed hidden qualms while simultaneously releasing peace.
With every conversation, a new page is written
And the shattered, tattered, and torn pages of what once was
Is disintegrated back to dust.
Deciphering fact from fiction has become a battle because this can't be
real.
Too good to be true.
Meanwhile your energy dances across the pages, introducing new
chapters.
To be continued…

Looking confused, Remy asked, "Who is she talking to?"

THE END

ACKNOWLEDGMENTS

I hope you all enjoyed my debut novella. Kalyani and Aeson are my first literary babies, but definitely won't be my last. I'm so glad Kalyani decided to set her hurt aside and give herself a chance to heal and explore the possibilities with Aeson. Aeson knew what he wanted from the start, but it took a lot of patience and understanding to hold on to his faith despite Kalyani's inconsistencies. Overall, they truly compliment one another, and I'm glad they helped each other heal.

Stay tuned for Esmee's story next…

Being apart of the "Seduction in Red, White, and Blue," collaborative, this has been quite a journey. Eye opening, informative, and very fast paced. This novella was written in two months! Can you believe it?! I've been "working" on my first novel for four years but managed to push out a novella in two months! I truly do work best when my back is against the wall, and the pressure is on.

To **everyone** who *genuinely* encouraged, supported, and poured into me during this entire process, I love y'all. I have gained some great connections with my SIRWB sisters, of course, our writing coach Robbi Renee! Thank you for the vision and connecting us and for helping me bring my vision to life!

If you haven't done so, please follow me on social media
   IG and FB: Juri Hines
   TikTok: Juri Hines_Writes

Also, please be sure to check out the remaining six books of the collaborative:

- **Fire & Ice** by Robbi Renee ~ *coming soon*
- **Now & Forever Free** by Subira Miles
- **Freedom is Mine** by M.K. Seven
- **Ignited on the Fourth** by The Author Cadence James
- **Star-Spangled Swagger** by Kamyra Harding
- **Smoldering Embers Still Burn** by Elle Robs

For all the music lovers like me, I couldn't write this book without the right soundtrack blasting through my speakers.
   Take a listen and enjoy the vibes!
   Spotify
   Apple Music

Made in the USA
Columbia, SC
11 July 2024

38510165R00070